Hawks Crossing

Sandra Marek Behringer

Kris,
Thanks for your help researching John's Rasor family line.
Hope to see you on another trip to Rockport!
Sandra Marek Behringer
Autumn, 2010

Tate Publishing, LLC

"Hawks Crossing" by Sandra Behringer

Published in the United States of America
by Tate Publishing, LLC
127 East Trade Center Terrace
Mustang, OK 73064
(888) 361-9473

Scripture quotations marked "KJV" are taken from the Holy Bible, King James Version, Cambridge, 1769.

ISBN: 1-9331488-4-5

Dedication

This book is for John
for our children and our grandchildren
for my mother who lived to see it
and my father, Joseph Marek,
who did not

"Each of us is a falconer. The hawk we let loose from our fist may not be visible to the human eye but it is to the human heart. That hawk is unique—the part of us capable of flying high and wild, capable of hunting, capable of the kill. The name of the hawk we carry names the deepest part of us. One person lets fly love or recklessness, another anger or envy. Sensuality, healing, poetry, and music are hawks and so is prayer. For most of us there is more than one, though surely one among them is our most constant companion."

Maddy's Journal

LIST OF KEY CHARACTERS

Kate Brady, a young woman returning to a small, Indiana town to solve the mysteries of her life

HER FAMILY

Tessa Zahler McLaren, Mother of Emily & Madeleine; Kate's great-grandmother

David McLaren, Father of Emily & Madeleine; Kate's great-grandfather

Emily McLaren Gerard, Mother of Elizabeth & Jessie; Kate's grandmother

Edward Gerard, Father of Elizabeth & Jessie; Kate's grandfather

Madeleine McLaren, Kate's great-aunt, Emily's sister; Mother of Delores

Fredryk Bauer, A talented artist; Father of Delores

Delores McLaren, Madeleine's daughter by Fredryk Bauer; Kate's cousin

Elizabeth Gerard Brady, Kate's mother

Terry Brady, Kate's father

Jessie Gerard McCann, Kate's aunt, her mother's sister

Ben McCann, Jessie's husband

FRIENDS, NEIGHBORS, ENEMIES

Opal and Gene Krause, Jessie's neighbors

Kyle Krause, Opal's son by Edward Gerard

Greg Krause, Kyle's brother; Gene's son

Alice Munro, A widow who raised Emily and Madeleine

Kenneth Munro, Alice's son, married to Diane

Diane Munro, Kendra's mother

Kendra Munro, Kenneth and Diane's daughter; Alice's granddaughter

Billy Caine, Kendra's husband

Carl Caine, Kendra and Billy's son

Sissy Caine, Carl's sister

Marie Celeste Lenoir, Kate's best friend

Drew "Rhett" Butler, Marie Celeste's husband

Therese and André Lenoir, Marie Celeste's parents

Josiah Erhlmann, Husband of White Sky; Grandfather of John Erhlmann

White Sky, The Miami Indian woman who married Josiah

John Erhlmann, Josiah's grandson; a physician

Mike Collier, Kate's lawyer and John Erhlmann's nephew

Sharon, The woman with strange eyes and the gift of healing

Prologue

Kyle's head was pounding as he cradled Beggar into the pit he'd dug under the locust tree south of the barn. Very drunk and almost collapsing with the weight of the old dog, he cursed the driver who left Beggar as roadkill not five hundred feet from his driveway. Beggar was the last good thing he could remember before his life fell apart.

Kyle dragged his sleeve across his eyes. After he covered the carcass with dirt, he threw the shovel as far as his strength permitted and walked across the yard to the kitchen, slamming the screen door behind him. His ma had lit the lamp by the window and left a note for him on the linoleum tablecloth. He glanced at the scrap of paper then crushed it into a ball. So the ceilings in the upstairs bedrooms were leaking again. He couldn't do any more to fix the confounded roof and there was no money to hire it done. Life was rotten—had been for a long time. It hobbled his ma and cheated him. It had even taken the dog.

The man who had raised him and should have taken care of them was dead. He had been a soft man like his son Greg, Kyle's half-brother. Useless, both of them. Resentment spewed from under the thin skin of his memories: his hatred was a wound that never healed. He pulled the bottle of Seagram's from the box behind Beggar's bag of dog food. Ma had no truck with drink, but she never fed the dog and never found his stash.

Next morning, Kyle woke up face down in the roots of a catalpa tree, his mouth dry and foul. He spit into the ground and looked around for the bottle. It was an arm's throw away and empty. Kyle squeezed his eyes shut a couple of times to clear them and looked at his watch. It was almost ten o'clock. He'd have to make up another excuse for not showing up for work at the garage. Not that Brown wouldn't figure it out. Kyle knew he'd better be more careful about the drinking or he'd lose his job for sure. He glanced up at the almost cloudless sky but its brightness hurt and he shut his eyes. When he opened them again he was looking at the lopsided shed a few yards in front of him, a place he had liked to hide when he was a kid. Beggar would lie on the floor, his legs twitching in his sleep, while Kyle carved a totem or practiced throwing his knife at the knots in the log walls. Even before he knew Eddie was his father, he'd sneak into the shed and pretend it was his own place. It was, of course. All of it. The old white house you couldn't see from there and all the land around it was his too. But she owned it. The thought of her made him feel crazy. He wanted to hurt her. He could probably kill her. God help her if she crossed his path now. He got up and walked toward the shed to sleep it off. He stopped at the half-open door.

The child was asleep on a pile of blankets, her body curled into a ball, the puppy's full, pink belly pressed against her chest. Kyle leaned against the doorjamb and watched her. He reached into his shirt pocket for his pack of Luckys and fumbled for the matches in his jeans. He lit up and looked at Elizabeth's child through the smoke. She was a miniature of her mother. Kyle remembered Beggar's bloody head. Eddie had given him that dog. Now they were both gone. He thought about his mother's tight, white face and the way her limp made her twist when she walked. His head throbbed.

The child stirred in her sleep and Kyle's eyes were drawn to her little hand as it opened, her pink fingers uncurling around a box of matches. Watching that hand, his eyes narrowed and he was suddenly alert as though waiting for something. He moved into the shed and saw the candle stump she'd been trying to light. A few burned-out matches lay on the ground beside it. He frowned and stared at her, at the puppy asleep on its back, and at the small arm wrapped around a teddy bear.

He had waited a long time to find a way to pay them back. The child was the key. He could hurt her physically or cripple her innocence but there were rules about how a decent man behaved with children. And he was decent, even though he'd been cheated, denied what was his, and left unmanned.

Since the day Emily died and Eddie disowned him, Kyle never felt physical desire. Incapable of love, he was barely capable of sex. The whole thing disgusted him. He was planning to marry Donna, of course, because his mother wouldn't live forever and he would want someone to do for him. Donna was a nurse so she was smart but she was also nervous and not very attractive.

She wouldn't demand much of him and would do whatever he wanted. That was all he needed.

The idea leapt into his mind like a living creature. It expanded, filling every corner like the smoke from his cigarette. He'd been patient, waiting his opportunity, and now he knew how he would start to get his own back. He stooped down and reached for the little girl's shoulder, his lips parted in a thin, deliberate smile. Kate felt him shake her and turned her face into the blanket but he didn't stop. She forced her eyes open and sat up when she saw him leaning over her. Her eyes said that she recognized him and that she didn't like him. He thought her mother probably told her to steer clear of him. "Wake up, you little firebug. What have you been doing?"

Her eyes opened wider. "I was just playing. You won't tell mama, will you?"

"Like to play with fire, huh?" he asked. "Like to see it blaze up and swallow everything it touches?" He smiled when he saw that she was afraid of him.

"No, no." Her eyes opened in such innocence that he leaned back and almost changed his mind. She started to cry. I just wanted to try lighting the matches; I didn't want to burn anything."

He ground his cigarette into the dirt to give the anger time to well up in him. "Yes, you did, Kate. You wanted to see a little fire turn into a big one, maybe one big enough to burn down this shed."

She swallowed hard to stop her tears and her pink lips trembled. He had bent so close that she could smell his breath, stale from the liquor and cigarettes. He wanted her to smell it and to be afraid.

"You need a lesson, short stuff, or you might do something terrible with fire. Firebugs do bad things, you know. You have to learn that fire can hurt." It had been smart to say it that way. Then he did the thing he was proudest of, the best thing. He pulled the teddy bear from her and looked at it. Kyle held out the bear and she clutched it to her. "Look here, Kate, you have to make up for the bad thing you did. You have to light a match and hold it against your bear to learn how fire can hurt. You have to burn your teddy bear to be forgiven."

She was crying harder. "I can't hurt Timmy. He's . . . he's my bear. Mama gave him to me when I was a baby." The puppy pushed against her and turned over. Kyle watched her whimper and then he slowly, deliberately picked up the puppy. He held out the match box in his other hand.

"No, no. I won't hurt . . . hurt Timmy," she said and shook her head, tears running from her eyes and nose. Kyle lit a match against his thumbnail and gave it to her. Her shoulders were shaking with her sobs and her head drooped.

"Well, if you won't hurt Timmy then I'll just have to set fire to this little guy, won't I?" Her head jerked up and her streaming eyes were wide with terror. "No, please no, don't hurt Penny! You can't hurt Penny!" she sobbed.

"Kate, you have to choose. You're a firebug and you have to be punished. Will you put the match to Timmy or do I burn Penny's paw?" He had moved the match quickly under one of the puppy's soft pads and the puppy whined.

He watched her as she stared at the puppy and finally held out one small hand. He had won. Kyle lit another match and the child touched it to the brown fur of the bear. She was crying so hard she was choking. Acrid smoke curled into her face. She dropped the match when the flame touched her fingers. She stared at the bear with huge eyes, unable to look away from the black patches where the fur had burned.

Kyle stooped closer. "You're a bad little girl, Kate. First you played with matches and almost burned down the shed and then you burned your teddy bear."

"You made me, Kyle! You made me!" she said looking up at him, her face crumbling with fear and confusion. He stood up, towering over her. "You did it yourself, Kate. You took that match and burned your bear, didn't you? You wanted to see him burn. I think you will try to hurt other people with fire if you get the chance. You're a bad child, Kate, and you had better not lie and tell anybody that I made you do this. If you do, I promise you I will burn Penny until he's all covered with black places and crying like a pig. Remember that, little firebug." He knelt closer to her and whispered. "And I won't stop at the puppy. I'll burn you, too." The child's eyes were wide and staring, her pupils dilated.

Kyle picked up the burned bear. "Now don't worry, Kate, I'll bury your old bear and no one will know what you did. No one but me." He turned and looked at the child intently before he walked out. She stood with her head down, her thin shoulders still shaking as she cried. He dropped the puppy and the small creature yelped and ran out of the shed.

He walked back to the farm, grinning as he realized his headache was gone. Poor Elizabeth. She couldn't protect her little girl from him. Avenging the sins of the mother on the daughter was fun. He'd gotten some of his own back.

Kate

"Sorry I startled you, Miss. Please put your seat upright. We're about to land."

I struggled out of my dream and saw the stewardess move down the aisle. I could still feel the scream rising in my throat and arms tightening around me.

The wrinkled face of the man sitting in the seat by the window was intent on his book. At least I hadn't embarrassed myself by screaming out loud when I woke. Marie Celeste told me that I did that sometimes. While I tried to control my breathing, I focused on the worn leather book in his hands. It was a breviary. My first impulse was to turn away, uneasy about interrupting his prayers. That was just my old training kicking in since I hadn't prayed much in years. Still, I needed to talk, to say something, anything, to pull myself back to the safety of this moment and away from the dark place I had been. As I considered what to say, I looked past him out the window.

"Are you from Indianapolis?" he asked. Apparently he thought my turning meant that I was willing to talk. Like many people his age, he believed his years permitted him to open a conversation without concern for apparent rudeness. Usually that irritated me but at the moment I was glad for it. I looked into his broad face, florid under a thatch of silver hair. "No, I was born in southern Indiana, near Paoli."

"Orange County is a grand place." His smile spread wrinkles across his cheeks. "One of my nephews spent some time studying the karst there."

I was surprised that he knew about the karst. The memory of that place dispelled the last of my dream. When I was very young Grandfather and Aunt Jessie had taken me to see the limestone pool where water from an underground river bubbled through. They had taught me lots of interesting things. Like how to love them and then do without them when they abandoned me.

"I know about the karst," I said. The moment of healing dissolved into anger.

"Don't you find it interesting that the fish that live in the cave where the water surfaces are blind? I've often found that diminishment on the one hand opens the way to blessings. A great mystery to ponder."

"You're a priest, aren't you," I said, nodding at the breviary.

"Guilty as charged." Until then I hadn't recognized the Irish brogue that softened his words. "I'm returning from a bit of a vacation from my work. Went back to Dublin. FBI, you know." I shrugged and he smiled. "Foreign-born Irish," he said.

"Where is your parish?" I asked without real interest. I had to keep talking.

"Ah no, I'm no parish priest. I'm the administrator of a small retreat house in Louisville." He looked at me with another smile and bent his head to the side. "It's called Our Lady of Peace Retreat House. Perhaps you've heard of it if you're Catholic."

"Guilty as charged," I repeated. "Not practicing though," I added deliberately, hoping to discomfort him. "Is there something special about your retreat house?" I was barely listening

"Well, lately a few newspapers have written about our healing ministry." He continued to talk and an engaging smile moved across his mouth every time he caught my eye. It was hard not to like him, but liking people was not my forte. The only time I seemed to manage it was when I was around Marie Celeste or Drew. Anyway, I probably only imagined that the smile was directed at me. "Excuse me?" I said. His words had been lost in the sound of people around us beginning to unbuckle their seatbelts and preparing to deplane.

"I just asked if you agreed that sometimes people are like the karst, breaking through after being lost." His eyes held mine a moment longer than I found comfortable and I stood up. "No," I said, "that never occurred to me." I pulled my bag from the overhead compartment. As I turned to leave he smiled again. "God bless you, my dear." Not likely, I thought, as I moved down the aisle.

Arriving in Indianapolis I walked into sunlight splashing through expanses of glass that enclosed the gate areas. I stopped at a restroom, touched up my lipstick and fumbled in the Fendi leather bag on my shoulder for a comb. Delores had given the purse to me for Christmas. I leaned closer to the mirror, separating smooth strands of hair to check the color of my roots. The dark rinse made my blonde hair a deep brown. I smiled at the thought that my aunt and my grandfather would get a shock when they saw the face that stared back at me from the mirror. It was Elizabeth's face, especially now that I had changed my hair color to hers. My eyes had her heavy lashes and the same shape. "Cat's eyes," the girls in high school had called them. "Kate, the cat," Marie Celeste called me when I told her that. She said it as if those eyes made me exotic, mysterious. Well, given my history, I guess I was a bit mysterious, even to myself. I glanced in the mirror one last time. I have Elizabeth's slim body, too, I thought to myself. I tucked the silk tee I was wearing down into the narrow waist of my Anne Klein slacks.

I picked up the keys to a white Chrysler at the Hertz rental counter. After looking at the map, I drove east on 465 to highway 37 and turned south. Ten minutes into the flow of traffic the dream tried to crawl back inside my head. My fingers curled around the steering wheel. It was all starting again. My arms were pushing someone away, someone who was holding me too tight. Through eyes narrowed with the pain of a rising headache I saw the McDonald's sign and changed lanes.

Waiting in the drive-thru, I took a deep breath, making a conscious effort to relax. The bright pink nails of the girl at the drive-thru window gleamed against the Styrofoam cup she handed me. I put the steaming coffee in a holder between the seats and held out my hand for my change, turning away so she wouldn't see how much I disliked her for the easy way she expected me to return her smile. Marie Celeste was always trying to help me accept the contentment of people around me without resentment. After I pulled into a parking space, I blew on the coffee long enough to cool a sip and then wash down three aspirins. I estimated that I was at least two hours from Paoli.

Back on the highway, I glanced at myself in the rearview mirror. Behind the cool eyes of "Kate the cat" was a bewildered five-year-old who didn't understand why her parents had to die in a fire and why she was being sent away.

A green metal sign told me I was 46 miles from Bloomington. The Styrofoam cup was empty before the road became two lanes. I was driving past the stonecutters' town with its sprawling campus and controversial basketball coach. The scenery kept changing. Industrial buildings and car dealerships morphed into cornfields, views of tree-crowned hills, and pale, limestone walls. Sugar maple trees and some wrenched and twisted evergreens edged closer and closer to the road. Old photographs kept crowding my mind. Back home again in Indiana. What strange candlelight burned bright through the Sycamore for me?

I had tossed the photo album in the back seat of the Chrysler when I picked it up at the airport. Looking at those faces during the flight made me apprehensive and confused. The old priest had glanced at the photographs, and afraid that he would feel the need to ask me about them, I closed the album and put my seat back so I could try to sleep. That's when I fell into the nightmare. Thank God I hadn't screamed.

I touched the expensive strand of pearls around my neck. Marie Celeste had given them to me for being her maid of honor. The pearls conjured images of the candlelight ceremony in St. Louis Cathedral where my small, quicksilver friend had married the young man we called "Rhett." It had been a watershed for both of us. I leaned back in my seat, put the car on cruise control, and tried to remember all of it.

Tourists in Jackson Square had stared at Marie Celeste as she stepped out of her limo and stood on the steps of St. Louis Cathedral. I arranged the long, Alençon veil over her gown as their curious eyes admired her. Why shouldn't they? She was the crème de la crème of New Orleans society, the granddaughter of a famous carnival queen whom Frances Parkinson Keyes had used as a prototype for one of her books about the Crescent City. The fine, old lace of her heirloom veil covered my hands like fairy tale cobwebs. She was, after all, a magical, irresistible creature, the faerie queen. I smiled at my beautiful, dearest friend, who was about to marry the man I had hoped would love me.

After the nuptial Mass, when she left the cathedral on Drew's arm, there was spontaneous applause. A saxophone swung into "It Had to Be You." I think of that moment in Jackson Square whenever I hear it.

It was playing in my head when we arrived at Antoine's on Rue St. Louis. While we nibbled canapés in front of cases displaying vintage carnival costumes in the Proteus and Rex rooms, we moved more or less to the Dixieland beat of a jazz quartet. When we were seated for dinner, our meal was a celebration of French Creole cuisine including the famous Oysters Rockefeller invented by Jules Alciatore and Antoine's own Pompano en papillote. Champagne bubbled in my glass and the murmur of the crowd and the sight of my incandescent friend made me lightheaded. I was surrounded by some of her young cousins, handsome, dark-eyed heartbreakers in evening dress. She must have asked Charlie and the rest to be certain that I had a good time because they stayed at my side before, during, and after dinner.

When we left Antoine's, the celebration moved to the Lenoir's Garden District Home. I was dancing through the rooms on a wave of music and euphoria in Charlie's arms when the band began to play "As Time Goes By" and Drew shouldered his way through the dancers. "Here's looking at you, kid," he said, cutting in with an elbow for Charlie and a slow smile for me. "Of all the gin joints in all the world, she walked into mine and you were the one who brought her. Thanks, Katie." He leaned down and kissed my cheek. "Play it again, Sam," I said, turning my head. He smiled and kissed me again.

Before Marie Celeste fell in love with Drew, I had dated him for a year. Movie dialogue was one of dozens of small connections between us. In my memories of the time we spent together I always see us laughing and searching for new ways to communicate privately in a crowd. He was surprised and hurt when I began refusing dates, but once I knew Marie Celeste had her heart set on him I backed away. I owed her more than I could ever repay. Even my developing feelings for Drew fell before that banner. Of course, once he began dating Marie Celeste, he was enthralled. It was impossible for anyone to resist her. When they announced their engagement, I put my arms around both of them and accused her of marrying the only man meant for me. Moving to the music in his embrace, I knew that my teasing had sprung from a seed of truth buried inside me. Except for Marie Celeste, I would have tried to make him love me. But it was all history. Drew was deeply in love with her and I had accepted that reality long before the marriage vows were spoken. When the music stopped, he tightened his arm around me, brushed his mouth against my cheek and walked away. My cheek felt hot where his lips had touched and though Charlie came back to claim me and there were couples dancing all around us, I felt very much alone.

About five-thirty in the morning, our feet crushing petals

on the flower-strewn veranda, we waved the two of them off to their hotel room. The lights that spilled through windows and French doors went out. The music stopped inside me.

Back in my room at the Lenoir house, I shook off my sandals, removed my earrings, and stared into the mirror above the dressing table. Flushed from dancing and wine I might have been a member of Marie Celeste's warm, gregarious family. But that wasn't the truth. As I leaned closer, I could only think about Elizabeth. The resemblance was strong.

I slipped out of my silk gown and opened the closet door. Pulling the cord to turn on the light, I looked up and saw a shaggy toy wedged into a corner of the shelf. I began to tremble and shut the door with shaking hands. My heart was pounding and my breathing grew ragged. Something I couldn't remember made me react to teddy bears with mind-numbing terror. Here, in the safest home I had ever known, the humiliating phobia had surfaced again. Would the dream return, too? The dream was worse. The cloak of sophistication I had tried to keep in place fell away and I wrapped my arms around me, shut my eyes and willed away my panic. When I was in control again, I decided to change my plans. I didn't sleep, afraid the dream might return. Instead I sat in the small boudoir chair beside the bed, rocking back and forth. Hours later it was clear to me. I always knew that someday I would have to reclaim my childhood in Hawks Crossing and face my fears. I just hadn't known it would be now.

After seeing Marie Celeste and Drew off on their honeymoon flight, I cancelled my plane tickets for Paris. I wasn't sorry to disappoint Delores—just because she enjoyed my company now didn't change all the years I had felt her coldness and benign indifference. Lately I had begun to search for ways to be disagreeable and this change in plans would further frustrate her recent attempts to improve our complicated relationship. I made new reservations.

Anyway, the trip to Paris was just another in a meaningless series of gifts that Delores had given me through the years, this time occasioned by my graduation from Northwestern University. I dialed the number of Cherie's Salon where just two days earlier Marie Celeste and her bridesmaids gathered for manicures, pedicures, and hairstyling. I had something different in mind today.

For the last four years, I've lived in Marie Celeste's world. She shared André and Therese with me, the mother and father who gave their daughter's friend the love she had been denied since childhood. I visited their elegant Garden District home so often that one spring evening after dinner, when we were enjoying chicory coffee and the soft, deliciously flower-scented breeze that was entering through the French doors, André presented me with a key to one of their guest rooms. They even attached a magnolia shaped tile inscribed with "Katie's Room," to the door. That night my tears of joy and gratitude were diluted with those of loss and self-pity. Such kindness only made my misfortune more awful.

From the first day I met Marie Celeste in the Northwestern Union, when we inadvertently sat at the same lunch table, I wanted to be her friend. The untroubled joy in her eyes filled empty places inside me. There was a freshness about Marie Celeste, her clothes, her clear white skin, the clean lines of her body and the lavender scent that you breathed when she was there. Now that she's married to Drew Butler and they're off on a European honeymoon, I'm going back to the emptiness that always waits to swallow me. Well, life with Delores has prepared me for that.

Marie Celeste had put her arms around me before she boarded their plane. "Katie, I'll write as soon as we're back. Promise me you'll come for a long visit." Her Audrey Hepburn eyes were shiny with tears when she said good-bye. The tears were for me. She didn't know who would keep me from drowning in my own waters when she wasn't there to throw me a lifeline. I laughed and had enough self-control not to tell her where I was going. She would have hated what I wanted to do just as she would have been horrified to see me with dark hair. Marie Celeste hated any kind of deceit. Anyway, I was getting good at being left alone. It was my natural state. But I would miss the only person in my life who called me "Katie." It would never in a million years have occurred to Delores that I might prefer it.

Sometimes I can't believe that Delores is my cousin or that she cares for me at all. She is an artist like her father Fredryk and almost twice my twenty-two years. I was seven when Delores gave me the photo album that lay on the back seat of this rental car. At the time she had been helping me furnish a dollhouse with delicately carved pieces from the workshop of a miniaturist who was one of her few friends. In her sporadic attempts to do the right thing, she took me several times to the Thorne Rooms exhibit at the Chicago Art Institute. I always considered those beautiful rooms my personal possessions. I would stand staring at them for a long time, imagining people in those rooms, happy people who were a family. Hence the dollhouse, the only toy I ever asked her to buy. On one particular day, watching me with unusual intensity, Delores put down the tiny armoire she was holding and took my hand. I looked up at her in surprise. Physical contact between us was rare. She took her father's antique watch out of her pocket and began to rub the rose gold locket that hung from its chain like a shining charm. It was a habit of hers. She would run her fingers over the smooth gold whenever she was nervous or pained. Delores was all the family I really had, and her mannerisms were important to me. They were predictable and made me feel a little safer, like a story a child reads over and over; knowing it will always end the same way. At seven, I already knew that wasn't how life worked. Some stories have chapters, even endings, missing. My life was that kind of story.

"Kate," she said, "I have something to give to you."

"Is it a book?" I was a voracious reader and she fed my hunger. It was the one thing we did together in the evening. In my child's heart I wondered if it might be her way of showing affection for me. She read aloud from Malory's Le Morte D'Arthur and Charlotte Bronte's Jane Eyre. One Christmas Eve I lost myself in the world of the March sisters when I should have been sleeping. I took the books but I never really believed in the love they supposedly represented.

"It is a book, Kate, a book of your inheritance." When she grew emotional, she would stammer, the words sometimes frozen on her lips, then breaking out in puffs of air. "Come up to the studio and I will show you." She drew her cashmere cardigan tightly around her and went to the stairs.

Until that day, I had sometimes liked Delores despite her cold ways and hurtful words. I might even have loved her, if I had felt safe enough to love anybody. I followed her tall figure up the stairs to the third floor. A large skylight enhanced the light that poured through the wide windows of the studio. An easel in the middle of the room held an oil portrait of a Supreme Court Justice. The face of Mayor Richard Daley stared at images of other Chicago politicians, educators and society leaders that were hung or propped against the walls in various stages of completion. Delores was capable of working on several commissions simultaneously. I was to learn that hers is a large and remarkable talent, not as celebrated as her father's, but much admired nevertheless. I had known her to work through many nights, so engrossed that she didn't stop until morning reminded her that a new day was about to make its demands. I wasn't one of those demands.

I curled into the corner of the small loveseat where she sat and drew my legs up under me, sitting close to her but not too close, avoiding the contact I knew would make her withdraw. The thing that could still bring hot tears to my eyes was her habit of pulling away from my touch. She picked up a leather album that I remembered instantly. In my excitement I started to say something but Delores put a finger to her lips to silence me. She opened the book and for the next hour, I stared at photographs of Tessa and David, my great-grandparents, Emily and

Edward Gerard, my grandparents, and my great-aunt Maddy, Grandma Emily's sister. I studied the photographs of Aunt Jessie and Uncle Ben and touched the young faces of my mother and father, Elizabeth and Terry, which smiled up at me from a world that had disappeared. My eyes began to burn and I was afraid she would see me cry. Delores moved toward me ever so slightly, then leaned back and closed her eyes.

After I had squeezed my eyes shut several times and stopped the tears, I began to turn the pages, careful not to touch her arm. She opened her eyes as I was studying the photo of a thin woman with a fragile, captivating beauty. The woman's hair was as fair as mine. Delores touched the photo and stared at the woman for some time before speaking. My heart began to race in that unfriendly silence and I moved back into the soft cushions as though for protection. "She was your great-aunt Maddy," Delores said. She kept staring at the photo, almost as though she had forgotten that I was there. "She was my mother."

"Kate, you know that you were born in Indiana, not here in Chicago. When you came to live with me after your parents died in a house fire two years ago, you were five years old." She hesitated and for a moment I thought I saw a look of pain in her eyes. She looked away from me and continued to talk in her quiet, deliberate way. "After that happened, for a very long time you were sad because you were missing your mother and father and your family. After the fire your grandfather suffered a stroke and could not take care of you. Your Aunt Jessica also had to spend some time in a hospital. She asked me if you could come live with me until she was better and you could go back to her. I agreed but, of course, I knew that time would never come. Promises made to women and children are easily broken. But I let you believe them because you were so young. Well, Kate, you're old enough to hear the truth. You're here to stay and I'm all you have left of your family. We're stuck with each other." The smile that accompanied her words was stiff and cold.

I could not grasp the full impact of her words, but she

frightened me. I tried hard to call up the memories I had clung to when I first came to her . . . memories of falling asleep on the porch swing where I was curled up in mama's lap . . . the sun on my back when I rode with Daddy to Grandfather's house. I remembered the old tree that reached up to Grandfather's window. Sometimes Daddy would lift me onto one of its thick branches and I would play pretend while they sat on the porch and talked. Sometimes I would see the glow of the end of Daddy's cigarette when it began getting dark. How could Grandfather and Aunt Jessie think I would be happy with Delores? Her heart and her eyes were as empty as her cold house. I had been back to Hawks Crossing for one brief visit and afterward every night for months I cried myself to sleep. What had I done to be punished like this? I prayed to be forgiven. I prayed for the letter that would come to call me back.

My seven-year-old mind collapsed into the darkness of what she was saying. There would be no letter. Something happened to me as I sat there. A steady stream of tears wet my cheeks though I made no sound. My chest felt strange and cold. Delores looked at me for a long time and shook her head. "Now you know what the world is like, Kate. Never forget it. Do you remember when you and I went to visit your grandfather and your aunt? Jessica was better but wanted you to stay with me until she could come for you. For a long time you cried so hard when you looked at the pictures in this album that I decided to put them away. It's yours now. You can stay here with me as long as you want to, Kate. When you're older, you will decide how long that will be." I didn't answer her but I grew hot with the hatred I felt for her because she had kept that album from me. I had missed those pictures and begged her to find them when she told me the book was lost. I promised myself then that I would leave her as soon as I was old enough to be on my own. I would never, never come back.

Delores turned back to the photo of the delicate girl with long blonde hair. She had forgotten me again and spoke softly, as if to herself. "She was my mother and he always spoke of her as his dear love. But he never married her." My curiosity got the better of my anger. "How could he be your father if he wasn't married to your mother? If she had his baby wouldn't that be a sin?"

Delores leaned down close to me and her eyes were very cold. "Oh, yes, it was a sin, Kate, but the bigger sin was that when she was dying she had to leave me in the care of Judith Kelley, because my father had another family. I guess I didn't look much like my mother so it was easy for him to leave me." It was true. I looked more like her mother than she did, especially because of my hair.

"He sent money to buy this house and paid Mrs. Kelley to take care of me. When I was a child, he would come to see me from time to time. He set up a studio in this house and when I was little I would watch him paint. Sometimes I would sit on that stool, my hands on my knees, and watch him as he painted me. He sold that painting. I always wanted it because it made me remember him looking at me. On some of his visits, he taught me to paint. He said I had his talent and promised that one day we'd be together, two painters who would be very famous. Of course, he never kept that promise. He died and left me this house and his pocket watch." She looked up and I was afraid of the look in her eyes, even though she wasn't looking at me.

"So don't believe in promises, Kate. As long as you're in this house, we'll never make promises to each other. That way we'll both be safe from the pain they bring."

Delores left me with the book and later found me asleep with my head on Elizabeth's picture. When she tried to take the album from me, I woke and slapped her hand. She looked at me with a half smile on her face, or perhaps it was a grimace of pain. After that, I don't recall crying anymore when I looked at the album. The feeling growing inside me wasn't sadness but anger. Beyond the anger was the face of something else, something unspoken that frightened me most of all.

Just as Delores said, I never went back again to Hawks Crossing. Never until today. There were letters and a few photographs from my Aunt Jessie through the years, but with each year my memories of Hawks Crossing seemed more like a story in a book than part of my own life. There was an empty feeling inside me. I wrote less and less. I hoped they could tell I did not need them anymore, did not love them for sending me their unwanted presents on my birthday and at Christmas. One year they sent me a small tea set and two tiny dolls to share it. I went into my room, smashed the set, put the pieces in a bag and threw them into the trash. I gave the dolls to girls at school. Delores never asked me what had become of the toys.

I tried to forget Hawks Crossing, but it wouldn't leave me alone. I began to suffer from an awful, recurring dream and, sometimes, I woke up in another room; once in the yard. Hidden in that dream, I believed, was the secret of what I had done, the reason I was sent away from Hawks Crossing.

Delores told me my parents were Catholic so she enrolled me in a parochial school. What passed for my childhood spilled over into adolescence and high school. All through my years at Our Lady Academy I was a loner, filling my days with books and the records I played over and over. That music filled me up and stopped the hurt. I remember Ravel's Bolero. I locked the door to my room, played the bolero and danced and danced.

I dreaded events when parents were invited to meet the teachers and never asked Delores to take the place of Terry and Elizabeth. I always thought of my parents by their first names. You're free to do that with strangers who desert you. I would kneel in the small chapel with its gold trimmed gothic altars and stare at the face of the Madonna, her eyes cast down and a gentle smile on her lips. I said her rosary, and begged her to remember she was all the mother I had. But as my anger grew, the awful feeling kept choking me. I went less often to the chapel. The small, golden door of the tabernacle seemed locked against me. After a bit I didn't feel the presence of God in the Eucharist. I stopped taking communion. Then I simply forgot how to pray. Mother Alureda, one of the older nuns, saw my trouble and tried to comfort me. She died at Christmas, my freshman year. I was alone again.

My happiest years were spent in the drama program at Northwestern University on the shore of Lake Michigan. Before we graduated, my best friend, Marie Celeste Lenoir, asked me to be her maid of honor. She was planning to marry Drew "Rhett" Butler, the engineering student I had dated before she fell in love with him our sophomore year. Delores had planned to take me with her on a business trip to Paris after my graduation but I told her that I had to be in New Orleans for their wedding. I was glad to tell her that because I knew Delores had begun to enjoy my company and was looking forward to taking me on her trip. She asked me to join her after the wedding but instead I booked a flight to Indianapolis and then called the Hotel St. Louis on Ile St. Louis where she was staying and left the message that I would be visiting Aunt Jessie instead. It would have been satisfying to see the look on her face when she got the message.

I made an appointment to have my hair darkened. The stylist tried to talk me out of making the change. He said most women would pay him to give them that shade of blonde, but most women didn't have to settle an old score and face an unknown truth about themselves.

The farm lay between the towns of Orangeville and Paoli but I decided to ignore the sign to Orangeville. I wanted to drive into Paoli to see the old Greek Revival courthouse that was one of my few memories and, after driving the roundabout, take 150 W. Aunt Jessie had written the directions to her house in one of her letters. It was the only one I had kept.

My attention shifted to a dilapidated farmhouse on my left. An apple tree beside it reached to its roof just like the one I remembered climbing at my grandfather's old farmhouse. For a moment I thought I saw a woman standing at an upstairs window with her hand pressed against the pane. That face kept inserting itself into my thoughts, and when a swirl of yellow leaves hit my windshield, I felt dizzy for a moment. I tried to ignore it.

The white courthouse with its clock tower was just ahead of me. I barely managed to turn right and park before I slipped into the dark weakness that was rising up to meet me. I have no idea if I was asleep or unconscious nor for how long. When I lifted my head from the steering wheel, the dizziness I had felt was almost gone and I got out of the car to walk a bit.

I was parked in front of a small shop where a sign with the painted image of a pie safe hung above the door. On a whim I turned the doorknob that was part of a pattern of vines and leaves carved into the heavy wood. A bell jangled. Just inside on a marble stand was a brass art nouveau statue of Diana the huntress, her dog at her feet and her hand holding a broken bow. I did not miss the irony of that greeting, that recognition of one huntress by another. Both broken. On the wall behind the statue, pillowcases trimmed with tatting hung from pitted brass rods, like the draperies of a stage. As if on cue, the notes of a Chopin waltz rained softly around me. Following the music toward the back of the store, I passed a doll with long, dark hair. I took it from the cushion of a mission rocker and stroked the silky, faded champagne dress. I wondered what mother had given her daughter such a beautiful doll and what had become of that little girl. Delores had given me Madame Alexander dolls when I was little, and they were more expensive ones than this. They weren't to be played with, of course, just to be looked at on their shelf above my bureau. I put the doll back on the rocker with more gentleness than I had shown to mine.

Light glinted off ruby glass and I could smell the dust from a pile of books. WHEN KNIGHTHOOD WAS IN FLOWER was printed in gold on the blue leather jacket of a large volume. I opened it and read a few sentences embedded on yellowed pages. Another shelf displayed pressed glass goblets and willow china. Above it a woman's face looked down at me severely from a mahogany frame. For just an instant a wave of nausea threatened.

I kept walking. A beaded dress hung on a dressmaker's dummy at the back of the shop near a brocaded chaise. A phonograph was spinning Chopin's web of music from a roll top desk and beside it, steam curled from coffee in a thick, white cup.

Just to my right in a glass case, crystal earrings, costume jewelry, and garnet brooches glittered. A small distance from the trinkets, I spotted a rose gold locket with a velvet cord coiled around it. When I leaned in to take a closer look at the locket, the dizziness overpowered me and I had to steady myself with both hands on the glass to keep from falling.

"Are you all right?" I felt rough hands on my arms. Just before I fainted, I smelled cigar smoke.

I was lying on the chaise looking up into the deep blue blur of eyes above a coffee cup. The man's brown hair was pulled back into a ponytail and he was studying my face with a somber earnestness that embarrassed me. I dropped my eyes only to have them rest on the powerful shoulders and arms visible through his white tee shirt. His mouth was half hidden in his well-trimmed beard. "How are you now?" His voice was low and rough, the kind people call "whiskey voice." A sudden headache like a fist to the back of my head took my breath. I closed my eyes again until the tension broke and I could speak normally.

He put down his coffee and poured a glass of water from a ceramic pitcher. His eyes never left my face as he waited for me to speak. "I don't know what's wrong. I've come down with a virus or something." The tone of my voice was annoyed, unfriendly. I could tell by his expression that that fact wasn't lost on him.

He held out the glass of water in a hand covered with fine sawdust.

"That won't be necessary," I said as I raised my hand to reject the water. "I parked in front of your shop because I felt faint. When my head cleared, I decided to have a look. Sorry to be so much trouble," I added grudgingly. He continued to hold out the glass, so I took it and sipped the water, unable to think of anything else to say and aggravated with myself for feeling the need to explain. "Thank you, Mr. . . ."

"Carl. I'm Carl Caine."

"Thank you, Mr. Caine. I'm fine now. I'd better get back on the road." As I rose to leave, he held out his hand. It closed around mine in a hard grasp and pulled me effortlessly to my feet. He released my hand a second later than I expected and I felt my pulse quicken.

I decided to pay for his help with a purchase. "I think I saw a piece of jewelry in this case that I'd like." He looked at me with an expression so fleeting I could not identify it. I wondered if I would have to pay dearly for my generous impulse.

"Would it be this?" He reached into the case and took out the rose gold locket. It seemed smaller in his hand. I took it from him.

"Yes. That's it. How did you know?" For a moment, he seemed uncertain. "I thought I saw you looking at it before your spell," he said. "It's thirty dollars."

"I have better, though." He reached under the counter and opened a box with an unremarkable cameo inside. "This piece has a fourteen karat gold chain." I looked at the delicate piece and smiled. He noticed and returned the favor.

"I'll take it."

A trace of his smile lingered as he spoke. "Seventy-five dollars for that."

Just the thing for Aunt Jessie, I thought. My turn to give her an expensive, meaningless present to repay her for all the gifts she had sent instead of sending for me.

"Yes, I'll take it, but I want the locket, too," I added quickly as he closed the case. "Does it open?" Somehow I knew it did and that when it was opened I would recognize a thin face framed in dark hair.

He watched me put my thumbnail into the narrow space between the sides of the case. The locket was empty. My surprise and disappointment must have been obvious. He looked at me with the intensity I had noticed before. "Did you hope someone had left something in the locket?"

The face was clear in my mind. "It seems as though I did." I said, fighting a feeling of panic. Why should I have any inkling of what was inside that piece of jewelry, when I had no clue as to the person who lived inside my own head? When he took my money and wrapped the jewelry, a woman came out of the back room. The deep-set blue eyes and dark brows were like his. Mother and son for certain. As she looked at me, her expression grew slack and I could feel her dislike as palpably as a hand on my skin. It shook me for a moment. When I turned to leave, I heard him say, "It's all right, mother." I opened the door and did not look back.

I felt his eyes as I walked past the window and wondered why that bothered me. A handsome man and I had met briefly and instead of finding the incident intriguing, I wanted to run away, like a little girl frightened by a shadow on her bedroom wall. I smiled at the idea that a bedroom entered into the picture at all! What did it matter? I'd never see him again, I thought, with just a twinge of regret. The woman, his mother, wouldn't regret it at all. I wondered what there was about me that roused the immediate and powerful dislike I had read in her eyes.

Before leaving for the farm, I decided to walk the square. Although I remembered little from my early years, I did have a memory of climbing the cannons at its entrance. I glanced through the glass door of the historical society and, from her desk, a woman with reading glasses on the end of her nose, smiled at me. I smiled back and walked a bit further, passing a restaurant, the office of an attorney, and a hardware store. I could hear people talking and the companionable sound of laughter. I was surprised by the strong desire to forget my purpose and to become just another visitor to this small town. It didn't last.

I was eager to be on my way. I wanted to see the look on Aunt Jessie's face when I came to the house. When I told her who I was, I would tell her this wasn't a social call. I'd demand that she tell me why they didn't want me and what I had done that caused them to send me away. Since my grandfather had a stroke after the fire, I wasn't sure he could understand what I wanted or have enough speech left to answer my questions. But she could. Aunt Jessie could. I would tell them that I sincerely hoped that they would be punished for what they had done to me. Then I would go away and never see Hawks Crossing or them again. I wouldn't let them see how afraid I was or break down in front of them, no matter what they might tell me. I would go away and lose myself in another place and deal with it. Anger was filling all the empty places inside of me. My fervent hope was that seeing me again would destroy their peace of mind for the rest of their lives. I wanted to spoil their lives and rob them of happiness. I wanted them to live without it as I had for so many years. I wanted them to know the bitter taste of loneliness.

I opened the car door and slid behind the wheel. Taking the rose gold locket from its bag, I fastened it around my neck. It slipped under my tee and I felt its chain and smooth oval against my skin. I backed out carefully, waiting for a chance to enter the stream of cars. I took the next turn, traveled west on 150 and watched for the cemetery by Ames Chapel where, just as Aunt Jessie had described it, the headstones reached almost to the road. I turned right past the small brick building with its bell tower surmounted by a cross. A few miles farther, near a patch of woods, I saw the shell of a gray barn. Horses walked along a fence, noses in the grass, except for an old mare gazing at me, unmoving as a statue. "Sorry, old girl, but it's not Elizabeth. It's Kate."

Bittersweet vines twisted over fences and down into ditches filled with white Queen Anne's Lace on its stiff stems. I was like that, stiff and straight under patterns of life I couldn't explain even to myself. I lost track of time as I drove, stopping only once to check the map. It was late afternoon, with five o'clock shadows growing longer on the grass. The narrow road rolled through the fields, then curved. I became aware of a stream widening beside the road. Lost River. Its name was written on the back of an old black and white photo in my album.

A pair of hawks circled over a farmhouse set far back from the road, its long driveway lined by a wire fence and a few old catalpas. Gravel crunched under the tires and its rising powder dulled the paint on my rental car as I turned down the long drive. I hit the brake for a moment to look at my aunt's house. White paint had peeled from the gingerbread of the porch and a wooden swing hung on rusted chains. It was the house I had looked at in photographs so often that I knew each feature by heart.

The front door opened and a woman stepped out. I took a deep breath and leaned out the window to call to her, aware of an unexpected rush of excitement as I anticipated the look of surprise on her face. The woman on the porch moved forward out of the shadow of the roof. Instead of my Aunt Jessie, her neighbor, Opal Krause stood on the porch. A sudden, sharp memory came to me. I remembered that she made my Aunt Jessie cry one day when she said something about her mother. In the child's heart still beating inside my own, I was afraid of Opal Krause. Was that why I remembered her name? I got out and slammed the door, catching the edge of my sweater. She stared at me without speaking. "What's wrong?" I said as I struggled to open the door, a clumsy child again to those critical eyes. "What's happened?"

The thin lips parted and her eyes stared. She couldn't hide her shock at my appearance. I felt a sense of satisfaction and power. After a moment her expression changed. She drew herself up, looked at me and paused before she spoke. It was a mannerism that made me think of a predator anticipating its attack. "It's Elizabeth's girl. Kate, isn't it? I would know that face anywhere. After all these years, you finally came back. You took your time about coming here. It's always that way. They never come until too late." The look in her eyes was accusing me of something. "Edward . . . your grandfather had a bad spell last night." For a moment, I thought she sounded genuinely saddened. "Jessie took him to the hospital." The thin lips tightened when she spoke my aunt's name.

She moved down the stairs with an awkward gait as I turned back to the car. "No use. They won't let you see him. Doc said no visitors tonight. It was another stroke, Doc says. His mind is gone."

I was filled with a sense of panic. That couldn't happen. Not now. Not when I was close enough to ask him all the questions that had built up in me over the years. "It was a bad one, Doc says. No use trying to put a good face on it." She walked past me in the direction of her house. "There's some chicken in the frigerator that's still good. Probably left over from what she had last night. I was going to take it but you might as well eat it. Not much of a cook, your aunt. Like her mother. I'll fix something else for Kyle and me. Something more to our liking." I watched her skinny figure move across the field. Her gait was jerky, slowed by a slight limp. "Get out of here, you horrid old woman," my mind screamed. "You're enjoying all this. I don't know why, but you are."

The house was exactly as I knew it would be from the photos in my album and maybe from some deep childhood memory. I entered a small hallway and ran my hand along the curved wooden banister of the stairway in front of me. To my left was the "parlor," as Aunt Jessie called it in one of her letters. A dark print of the "Night Watch" hung over the 1850s fireplace. I walked on wide plank floors to a camelback sofa and sat down, my fingers moving across the smooth fabric patterned in bright cabbage roses. A thin, fringed lampshade stood on a chest beside the sofa.

I took in the rest of the room slowly. A coffee table, its painted top protected by glass, held a clear vase filled with bittersweet and two stems of Queen Anne's Lace. A jumble of books was visible behind the glass doors of a bookcase decorated with exquisite carvings of dogwood blossoms. The Philco radio beside a rocking chair released an old memory. "It's a piece of history," I remembered Aunt Jessie saying. "President Roosevelt's fireside chats came to me through that floor radio and I listened to Stella Dallas and I Love a Mystery on it." I didn't know anybody named Stella and wondered what the mystery was.

Walking into the kitchen, I looked at the table covered with a crocheted table runner and wondered if Jessie had made it. There was a black gas stove and a small Kelvinator refrigerator. A carpet beater hung on the wall near a small, framed picture taken at a church picnic. It was all very plain and uncluttered. A corner cupboard held the only surprise in the room—delicate bone china more suited to a formal dining room than a farmhouse.

I flipped the switch in a bath off the kitchen and the light spread across walls papered in a pattern of carousel horses. A dark bar of Yardley's old Lavender lay in a metal soap dish hung on the claw foot tub. Wide panels of lavender glass framed an oval Venetian mirror above the sink, reflecting a long, lace-covered window. The windowsill held a box of dusting powder decorated with lilacs. I had a small hand mirror of Venetian glass in our house in Chicago. It was a birthday present but I couldn't remember who gave it to me. It lay on the dainty dressing table in my bedroom. It occurred to me that this beautiful mirror could soon be mine. I shook the strange, unwelcome thought away.

Aunt Jessie had to stay well enough to tell me what I needed to know about my mother and father and the night of the fire. Then, when she tried to explain it all away, I would tell her I didn't want her or this place. I needed for her to hear me say that.

Her death was unthinkable. What I longed for was her presence, here tonight, in this house I had known as a child. I wondered how long I would have to wait before she returned home from the hospital.

Passing through the kitchen, I entered the small dining room. In its center stood a round pedestal table covered with a lace tablecloth and surrounded by six chairs. I wasn't surprised at the carvings of birds and leaves on their backs. It seemed to be a motif she favored. A braided rug covered the plank floor. A tulip lamp hung over it.

To the right of the stairway as one entered the house was the room I assumed was Aunt Jessie's bedroom. I walked to the iron bed and touched the wedding ring quilt. Her mahogany highboy and dressing table came from the old house in Indianapolis where Jessie had been born.

How did I know that?

A kidney shaped writing desk stood a small distance from the window seat. I could almost remember Jessie sitting at the desk, reaching for one of the books piled there. My eyes searched the room for anything else that stirred my memory. The vanity tray on the dressing table held perfume bottles and another small bouquet of autumn flowers but no recollections.

Two pictures hung above the tall dresser. Both women were young: One had dark hair and eyes and a petite figure. She stood on a stage in a long white dress, holding her diploma. The other face was Jessie's. Long red hair hung in curls to her shoulders, her eyes were wide and smiling even though her mouth was a prim, ladylike line.

I walked across the room and rested my head against the dresser. When the tears burned my eyes and fell in steady wet ribbons down my face, I moved to the bed and lay across it. The tears gave me a measure of relief and it felt good to let them come. After they stopped, I wiped my face and continued to walk through the house.

At the top of the stairs was the room Aunt Jessie said I

had slept in when I stayed overnight with her and Uncle Ben. I stared at the bed with its pink chenille spread. Everything was just the same as in a photo Jessie had sent me so "you won't forget Hawks Crossing, and your aunt." I looked at the faded print hanging over the bureau. Two people stood in front of an old brick house. The woman smiled down at the baby in her arms. The man in the fedora had his arm around her shoulders and his eyes met mine when I looked at him. The tears came again, hot and blinding.

I didn't open the door to my grandfather's room. Branches from the old tree that grew beside the house were brushing their leaves against the window of that room. Even now, as I heard the wind scrape them against the long, narrow window, I was filled with an aching sense of sadness and loss. I walked back to my aunt's bedroom and sat on the bed.

I woke to darkness pressing in on the bedroom window. It was complete, except where the sky was torn to display a slice of moon. I remembered where I was, and sat on the bed, wrapping her quilt around me, trying to feel her presence. Not fully awake, my anger faded and an unexpected and unacknowledged need for her surfaced. Aunt Jessie, I'm home and I have so many things to ask you. For the moment I gave in to that need.

I pulled the chain on the small brass lamp on the table beside the bed. A multi-colored pattern covered my hand and a small piece of the pillow. Wrapped in the quilt, staring at the jewel tones falling through the glass shade, I remembered a night when Aunt Jessie and I had cuddled close in this bed while she read to me from THE WIZARD OF OZ. In turn, she became the voice of Dorothy, the witches (good and bad), the munchkins, and Dorothy's traveling companions: the lion, the tin man, and the scarecrow.

Finishing the story, she shut the book with a firm thud, and took my chin in her hand.

"Katie, always remember, you can have anything you can believe in enough, anything you can want enough. But you have to be willing to give up everything else to have it."

I could still feel her small, warm hand stroking my cheek. I felt a slight chill as I realized that her touch was my own memory, not something she had written to me in a letter. I closed my eyes and remembered.

After the story, we sat in front of the fire, drinking hot chocolate which she served in small, flowered cups; the cups from the kitchen cupboard. Later, we sat on the swing and Ben joined us. I sat between them and fell asleep to the sound of their soft laughter and the creaking of the chains. The memory was really mine. I didn't bother to brush away the tears that slipped down my cheeks.

The sharp rings of the telephone startled me and with sudden, absolute certainly, I knew that my grandfather was dead. A woman's voice asked to speak to Mr. Gerard's granddaughter. The quiet voice told me there had been a fire at the hospital. The nausea that had filled my throat with bitterness at the antique store began to rise in my mouth.

By some miracle, I did not faint. "We have removed Mr. Gerard from his room. He was not overcome by the smoke, but his condition is still very serious. Mrs. McCann became so upset that the doctor has admitted her. She needs time to recover from shock."

"May I see her?" My voice was a dry whisper. Memory had made a coward of me. I was afraid of losing her.

"Of course. You are welcome at any time. You will be limited to ten minutes an hour, but you may stay in the waiting room as long as you choose."

"But I understood that Dr. Reuter had indicated no visitors at this time."

"Not at all. Family is always welcome in cases like these." I could see Opal's face, her cold eyes. "Yes, I must have misunderstood. How is it you knew to call me here?"

"We had a call a few hours ago from a neighbor, Mrs. Opal Krause. She told us you were at the house."

I wondered if she also told the nurse that she had lied to me about visiting my grandfather. "Thank you," I said, fighting my growing anger. "I'll come immediately."

Leaving the parlor light on, I shut the front door, slammed the screen door behind me, and slid into the front seat of my car. Switching on the headlights, I suddenly realized I had no key to the house. It didn't matter. All that mattered now was getting to see Aunt Jessie.

Backing out of the long driveway was a challenge, and I left some tire marks outside the gravel. Backing carefully onto the unlighted road, I headed for a gas station I had stopped at on my way to the house and got directions to the hospital.

I kept brushing away the tears I couldn't stop. I felt that I was not just driving through the night; I was driving through my fears to the source of my bad dreams.

The intensive care unit was on the second floor. A nurse wearing a pink flowered blouse over her white slacks looked up at me. The cheerful uniform belied her expression.

"Your grandfather is asleep. We have him on oxygen and intravenous fluids. The doctor is with your aunt. She was awake earlier and agitated, and he's giving her something to help her rest. I'll call you when the doctor leaves. Whatever you do, please don't try to waken her." She pointed to a line of chairs near the nurses' station. I sat in the nearest chair and waited for Dr. Reuter.

Half an hour later the nurse came to get me. The doctor was handling an emergency on another floor and would call me at home. He said that I could visit my grandfather and my aunt, but only for a few moments. I was not to try to waken them.

I nodded, and followed her to a door near the nurse's station. My grandfather lay in the shiny metal hospital bed surrounded by monitors, his body invaded by tubes delivering oxygen or attached to poles with bags of fluid. He was a stranger to me, this old man with his long, narrow face and deep-set eyes. He was another piece of my life being taken from me. Instead of resentment, sadness rose in me. "Hello, Grandpa Eddie," I said softly. "It's Katie, I'm sorry I've come so late. Please get better."

I entered Jessie's room, halfway down the hall. A thin, red-haired doll lay in the bed, moaning slightly as she breathed. My eyes filled with hot tears and my chest hurt. "Aunt Jessie," I whispered, "it's Katie. Please, please try to get better." I bent closer to her pillow. "Aunt Jessie, I need you."

The following day, I visited Grandfather and Aunt Jessie as often as hospital policies allowed. About eight o'clock in the evening Aunt Jessie opened her eyes and knew me. I put my hand under hers and she squeezed it. She closed her eyes and smiled, but seemed unable to gather the strength to speak. Then, after a few moments, she pulled me slowly toward her, and looked steadily into my face.

"Elizabeth, she's all right. I took care of her."

Her limp hand fell away from mine, and she went away into her dark, silent world. She had spoken to my mother, the mother I didn't remember, the mother who died in a fire when I was five. She was telling her I was safe. The person I had counted on to explain the riddles of my life was talking to my mother, not to me. I bent my head and gave in to the tears that burned my eyes. She closed her eyes and slept.

My grandfather died that night.

I opened the door to Jessie's house a little after ten o'clock. It was dark, but the deep sadness inside me, the sense of emptiness and loss, was greater than any fear of someone waiting in the dark to hurt me. And I was angry again.

Once inside, I walked through the rooms, switching on every light. Should my grandfather's departing soul be allowed one last look at his home I wanted him to see me there. I wanted to scream at him. "I'm still here and I still need to understand." I stood on the porch for a long time. When I was in control of myself again, I realized that I was hungry.

I found a can of Maxwell House coffee in the cabinet over the stove, brewed a pot, and took out the plate of chicken Opal had told me was in the refrigerator—the "ice box," Jessie sometimes called it. Jessie used to tell me about the icebox her parents had and how the man who brought the block of ice carried it on his leather-covered shoulder with large tongs. On hot, summer days, he would break some pieces from the block and she would suck the cold slivers until they disappeared into her warm mouth. I listened to her and felt it had happened to me. Another memory! Perhaps, here in this house, I would begin to remember more of the childhood I had lost.

I carried my sandwich and coffee out to the porch. Putting the plate on my lap and holding the cup carefully on the arm of the swing, I leaned back. Stars were brighter here than in Chicago where streetlights, neon signs, and the glow from thousands of windows dulled or obliterated them. A strong smell of honeysuckle drifted from vines twisting around the trellis at the side of the porch. Even the road was silent. Except for the cicadas singing in the trees and the creaking of the swing as it moved slightly with my weight, the night was very still.

The dark haired mother I couldn't remember probably sat here with my father, full of dreams that would blaze and disappear in the fire that killed them. That horrible fire had stolen not only Elizabeth and Terry, but Aunt Jessie's husband Ben. And it had changed and consumed my life.

One summer after I went to live with Delores she brought me back to Hawks Crossing. There were photos from that visit in the album. In one of them I am curly-haired and smiling, holding onto a tire, floating on a pond. But it was only a moment's respite. Jessie changed that summer. She didn't spend time with me or tell me stories. She was strange and distant, always reminding me to be quiet because Grandfather was sleeping or couldn't tolerate much noise.

There was one warm night when we were close again. We sat together on the swing with our thin nightgowns pulled up to our knees. The moon was very bright and she had her arm around me. She fanned us both with a white handkerchief while I snuggled against her, half asleep.

"Now that your mommy and daddy are in heaven, and Grandpa is so sick, we have to be brave, Katie. You'll have to live with your cousin, Delores, a while longer. Then, when Grandpa gets stronger, you'll come back and live with me." Her arm tightened around my shoulders and she put her head against my hair. I started to cry and when I looked into her face, I saw that she was crying, too.

"I don't want to go away from you, Auntie Jessie. I love you and Grandpa. And I miss you. Don't you miss me too?"

"Oh, honey, I miss you so much. But we have to wait a little bit longer before we can be together. Until I . . . until Grandpa is all well. I'll write to you and when you answer me we won't seem so far apart."

I stretched out on the swing; my head in her lap, looking up into her face and feeling lost and scared. The chains of the swing creaked as she slid her hand over my hair and hummed some wordless, sad tune until I fell asleep.

After I left Hawks Crossing, we wrote to each other at least once a month. I kept each letter in a box I decorated with little drawings of flowers and stars. Sometimes there was a long time between her letters and sometimes her handwriting looked shaky. She never said she would come for a visit though I begged her to come. Once or twice her handwriting was so strange it was as though someone else had written the letter.

What had happened? Why had I not seen her again until tonight? Why hadn't she ever come to see the little girl whom she said she loved but then sent to live in loneliness in cousin Delores' big house near Lake Michigan? Why hadn't I spent vacations in Hawks Crossing? Why didn't I know more about Elizabeth, my mother? What had happened the night of the fire? Now, when I came to demand answers to the questions that only she could answer, Aunt Jessie was too far away for my questions to reach her. Anger returned and with it came a strong resolve. Tomorrow when I talked to my grandfather's lawyer I would ask the questions that would help me piece together the puzzle of my life. My appointment was set for ten in the morning.

I shivered in the air that stirred suddenly and brushed my shoulders. It had grown cooler and darker. On the railing, the small, white faces of moonflowers opened. The faces of Elizabeth, Aunt Jessie, and my grandmother Emily glowed in the darkness of my memory. I had read about genetic memory. Could I access it? The darkness deepened around me and I decided to shake it off, go inside, and search the small attic off of my grandfather's room.

I was glad I remembered to retrieve the flashlight that lay on the kitchen counter. Bending to get through the small entry, I walked into the small, carefully organized attic. The beam of the flashlight played across boxes of various sizes, a few chairs, and a pile of books on top of a small chest decorated with chiseled designs. I removed the books and slowly brushed aside the dust around an exquisite, flower entwined carving of the initial M. Inside were packets of clothing wrapped in tissue paper, some letters, and at the bottom, several journals. The handwriting on the yellowed pages was rounded and clear. "Maddy's Journal" was written on the frontispiece. I flipped through the pages, appreciating the sketches of animals and birds that had been drawn by Maddy's hand. I stared for a little while at a superb rendering of a hawk. Beneath it, Maddy had written a reflection about the ways in which all men and women are falconers.

I held the journal against me and closed my eyes in a silent prayer of thanksgiving. Some of the secrets of my life were hidden in these pages. I was sure of it. Closing the lid carefully, I replaced the books on top of it, and then, carrying "Maddy's

Journal," I walked down to the kitchen to get more coffee. If it took all night, I would not go to sleep before I read every page of the journal.

Curling into a corner of the sofa, I placed the cup of hot coffee on the floor at my feet and opened the book. Maddy's writing was poetic. She pulled me along with her careful, Palmer method script but the day had sapped my energy. Just as I felt unable to keep my eyes open any longer, I came to her description of the trip she took with Emily and Eddie to visit his grandmother in Kentucky and I realized something important was happening in her life. And mine. As I read, the drowsiness vanished and my great-aunt Maddy commanded my imagination with her flawed, irresistible youth. The account of Delores' birth brought me to tears. There was so much I didn't know. There was so much Delores didn't know about the life of her parents. Worn out by the discoveries of the day and by the emotional shock of the journal, I fell asleep on the sofa.

The alarm on my bracelet watch woke me. I knew I had an appointment to keep, but for some minutes I lay there, staring at the ceiling, thinking about what I had learned from Madeleine herself. Putting the journal aside, I concentrated on a quick shower and change of clothes. Then I placed the call to Paris.

My cousin's voice broke. Our connection was good enough to let me hear the change. "Her journal? You will give it to me, won't you Kate? I mean, it really is mine." I was so stunned by the question that I didn't answer her for a moment. "You won't make me resort to an attorney, will you? I want that journal. It's mine! You must bring it back with you! No, wait. I can leave after I complete the photographs I'm taking for my portrait of . . . oh, never mind. You wouldn't understand its importance. I'll come just as soon as I can get away. I'll call when I reach New York so you will know about my connection to Indianapolis. Good-bye."

I stood there with the phone in my hand after we were disconnected. A speck of hope on my heart had just been scraped away. Nothing was changed. Had I really expected that we would become closer? Had I really wanted that? It would be strange to see her here in Hawks Crossing. But it seemed right, like completing a circle or hearing the click of a key unlocking a door. I glanced at my watch. I had ten minutes to make my appointment.

I looked up from the business card in my hand to the address on the old brick building on Main Street. His office was up a flight of narrow stairs. I turned the glass knob on his office door and light engulfed me as it poured in through an undraped bay window.

Someone was speaking my name. Lips moved on a pale face. Red hair curled around full cheeks. I felt the back of my knees against a wing chair. The arm of the chair was striped in burgundy and navy.

"Coffee?" I could smell the hint of hazelnut. "Thank you." The cloud settled deeper around me. Through it, Aunt Jessie was opening the screen door, waving from the porch. Wide, green eyes. Dimpled chin.

"Miss Brady," my name was repeating itself. I was in the waiting room of Mike Collier's law office, sitting on a camel back sofa facing the snowy farm landscape on the wall behind the secretary's desk. I recognized the work of Indiana artist Rob O'dell—snow falling against a dark barn and the tree beside it. Delores once bought an O'dell watercolor at a covered bridge festival she had visited in Parke County. She called my attention to his use of negative space. I understood that for the first time. I felt like negative space. I hoped there was a meaningful pattern around that space that I would someday understand.

The coppery head bobbed in my direction. "Mr. Collier is ready for you now, Miss Brady."

Michael Collier's smile was friendly and a bit quizzical. I was looking at steady brown eyes and sandy hair. It would be hard not to like someone who looked like Harrison Ford. The pleasant face frowned slightly and then he offered sympathy for my grandfather's death. The message in his voice was that he was somehow disappointed in me. I wondered why.

"I knew your grandfather all my life, Miss Brady, or may I call you Kate?"

I nodded. "Please call me Mike," he said and gestured to the chair beside the desk. I stared at the ornate carving on its outside panels and tried to remember something. His voice broke into my thoughts.

"Don't you remember me, Kate?" The smile had returned.

"I'm sorry. Should I? It has been a very long time since I left."

"Yes, of course. No reason why you should, is there?" The question seemed to require an answer, but I couldn't think of one.

"Although my father was his attorney, I often saw Mr. Gerard, your grandfather, here in the office and occasionally at my parents' home for dinner. They were great friends."

"I know very little about my grandfather, Mike. In fact, I know very little about my family. I was on my way home from the wedding of a classmate in New Orleans when I suddenly decided to try to remedy that situation." How long ago had I stood beside Marie Celeste, radiant in her grandmother's beaded wedding dress? How long had it been since the daughters of Garden District Society had moved unhurriedly into church in their elegant gowns beside their escorts in formal dress? I had felt a sharp stab of envy at her father's expression when he lifted the veil from his daughter's face. Marie Celeste's mother had squeezed his hand as he went to sit beside her. Had my parents ever looked at each other like that? I thought of Drew's face as he looked at Marie Celeste and couldn't resist surrendering to a feeling of despair. She was lovelier than the painting of her great-aunt Estelle, a great beauty who had once been chosen carnival queen of the Rex Krewe parade. The candlelight ceremony in St. Louis Cathedral played out inside my memory with the substitution of my face for Marie Celeste's under the Alençon lace of her veil.

"Kate?"

"I'm sorry. You were saying?" As I smiled at him, I was startled by the way his eyes moved across my face. He began to speak briskly and I wondered if I had imagined his scrutiny.

"I understand," he said. He opened a drawer on the credenza behind his desk and searched through the files. "Well. This is unexpected. Just a moment." He left the office. When he returned and was seated at his desk, he frowned again. "I can't explain this, Kate, but your grandfather's will is not in his file. My father was meticulous about paperwork." He glanced up at me. "Did I mention that he died last year? That's why I'm working with you." I murmured my sympathy.

"What happens if you don't find the will?" I asked.

"The laws of the State of Indiana will distribute the estate to his nearest relatives according to a formula that the law provides. That should not happen here though—I remember my father telling me that your grandfather had a will naming his remaining daughter Jessie as his heir and establishing a trust fund for you. I'm sure your grandfather kept his copy at the house."

Keep your trust fund, Grandfather, I thought. I wanted you not your money. Then I remembered something.

"The first night I came to Aunt Jessie's, before I went to sleep, I looked through my aunt's bookshelves. I noticed a manila folder on the shelf. Perhaps the will is in it."

"It's almost noon, Kate, and my two o'clock appointment has canceled. Why don't I take you to lunch, and then drive you to the house to help you recover the will?"

"Thank you, but I have to make funeral arrangements. Meet me at the house at two if that's convenient, and we'll search."

I thought he seemed disappointed as he stood and extended his hand. “I’ll see you there, Kate.” His touch was reassuring; as was the way he said my name. It would be easier to look for Grandfather’s will with him there.

A wine-colored Buick was parked in the drive when I returned from talking to Fr. James at St Agnes Church. We planned a funeral Mass following one evening of visitation for friends and family. It would be a closed casket visitation at the old Victorian mansion that was now the Hawks Crossing Funeral Home. I placed the picture of my grandfather and my grandmother Emily on their wedding day into the thin hand of the funeral director. It was a photograph I had found in my grandfather’s room that morning. Grandmother was very animated in the picture—her smile was wide and her head was tipped back against her husband’s chest. As I drove back to the house I wondered how much of her might live on in me.

Mike Collier was sitting on the porch swing, talking to a young girl in a white blouse and madras skirt. Her small feet were encased in brown sandals. I couldn’t see her face, but shiny, straight hair fell past her shoulders. Mike stood, took her hand and turned her toward me. The look that changed her face was one of recognition, a startled look that ended in a stare. For my part, I was equally shaken. A woman, not a young girl, stood there facing me, a woman at least ten years my senior, but a woman who seemed half child. She dropped her eyes and I was released from their extraordinary light. She turned them on Mike.

“Sissy,” Mike said in a soft voice, “this is Kate. She’s Elizabeth’s daughter come back from Chicago to see Jessie.” I walked up the steps and held out my hand. “I’m happy to meet you, Sissy.” She did not answer, but her eyes softened and she reached out to cup my cheek gently in her palm. I laid my hand against hers, moved by an illusive memory her face evoked. She smiled sadly and walked away, breaking into a little run as she drew nearer the bicycle propped up against Jessie's potting shed. Her figure was slight and again, from a distance, I thought she looked no more than twelve.

Mike looked at me questioningly. "You're early, and I haven't had lunch yet. Why not let me take you to our one and only corner restaurant. The food is good and the coffee's even better than mine. It's a good place to talk." When he smiled, I knew that was exactly what I wanted to do. I felt increasingly confused. Perhaps lunch would help me regain my balance.

The Main Street Café was a storefront coffee shop hidden behind the pots of Boston ferns and antique cookware that filled its plate glass window. When Mike pushed open the door, I could see a handful of tables covered with squares of blue and white oilcloth. In the center of each table was a carnation in a blue vase and a black plastic ashtray. The waitress was as old as Aunt Jessie. After we ordered our sandwiches, I cupped my hands around a mug of hot coffee and gave in to my curiosity about the strange woman whose eyes troubled me. "Tell me about Sissy, Mike."

He reached for the ashtray and took a pack of cigarettes from his shirt pocket. I declined his offer but nodded that he should go ahead. Mike struck a match, lit up, and inhaled slowly. For a moment I was alone. Just as the silence was becoming uncomfortable, his words floated like the smoke curling from the tip of his cigarette. "Sissy's a sweet girl. No, she's a sweet woman. Bright, too, but she hasn't spoken for years."

"What happened? What terrible thing did that to her?"

"You really don't know, do you?"

"Should I? I haven't been back to Hawks Crossing since I was five years old."

"No one has ever mentioned Sissy?"

"I live with my cousin and she's never spoken about her. My Aunt Jessie didn't mention her in any of her letters."

He leaned back and looked directly at me for a long

time before he spoke, his voice softer than before. He crushed out the cigarette inside the ashtray. "It was the fire, Kate. She hasn't spoken since the fire that killed your mother and father and Ben." A deep stillness filled me. Aunt Jessie used to tell me about the place where water seeped up through the limestone from a hidden river. It was called a karst and it was very near my aunt's home. She used to take me to visit the place where Lost River emerged from its underground bed. It came up through a cave where blind fish swim. I felt like those fish. For such a long time I'd been swimming in darkness. I looked up and realized that Mike was waiting for my question.

"Do you know about the fire? Can you tell me about it?" My voice had become a whisper, but I knew he heard me.

"I don't know much, Kate." He leaned forward, held my hand tightly in his a moment and then relaxed his grip. "Your mother and father were living in the Munro House. It's one of the oldest houses here at the Crossing," he added. "That morning I skipped school. My mother was fighting a severe attack of asthma and I was afraid that she was going to die. I needed time to be alone and a place where I could cry without someone else seeing me. I was heading for our cabin near the springs when I saw smoke curl into the sky. Then I heard someone screaming." He squeezed my hand again. "It was you, Kate."

I closed my eyes and tried to remember, but nothing came. Blind fish. Blind fish. Mike's voice went on.

"Sissy was kneeling in front of the house looking at the smoke pouring from a second floor window. She was holding you, pressing your face into her shoulder to stop your screaming. Your Aunt Jessie came running over to the two of you and yelled at me to get help. She told Sissy to go with me, but the girl just stood there, like someone hypnotized. She hasn't spoken since then. Doc calls it hysterical mutism. I came back with the fire truck and volunteer firemen. After awhile, I saw them carry out four bodies wrapped in blankets, and a small body wrapped in a towel." He looked at me with sadness and his hand stayed wrapped around mine in comfort. "That's what I know."

My dream. My terrible dream.

"Mike, was Sissy trying to stop me from running into the house? Or was she holding me after I ran out of it?" I heard the dead, cold sound of my question. Mike looked at me with something in his eyes I couldn't understand.

"I don't know. Kate." I thought he was going to say more but he didn't.

"Why, Mike? Why did it happen?"

Mike took both of my hands and chafed them. "Terry smoked cigars. The police thought that's probably what caused the curtains in the bedroom to catch fire. He might have fallen asleep in the chair while he was smoking. Sometimes . . . " Mike's voice dropped. "Sometimes he was a bit the worse for wear when he was depressed. He drank a lot, Kate, and the house was old, dry as tinder. Even a tiny fire would have easily gotten out of control. It was Terry," he repeated, looking deeply into my eyes.

So my father drank. I didn't remember that. I could barely remember him at all, just that he seemed very big to me. Perhaps I inherited my sense of insecurity from that man. Was that all there was to it? What could Jessie tell me about the fire? Was it just a terrible accident, compounded by her collapse when she learned that her husband had died trying to save Terry and Elizabeth? My mother died in that fire, I thought. Elizabeth was my mother. Somehow I could only think of her as Elizabeth

Aunt Jessie's face came to my mind. Was there a connection between the fire at the Munro House and the fire in Jessie's hospital room that worsened her condition and probably caused Grandfather's death? Was it more than a horrible coincidence that fire played such an essential role in her life and mine?

Mike was talking to me but I was so lost in my thoughts that I didn't hear what he was saying. "I'm sorry, Mike. I didn't hear you."

"I just wanted to know if you checked the bookcase. Was the will there?"

"No. I rummaged through all the books, but didn't find the manila folder I saw the first night I was in the house. It was a manila folder with navy edging and some typing on the tab. It's odd that I couldn't locate it. I'm sure it was there."

"You've just described the folders we use in our office, Kate. There's no question you saw one of them. Could you have moved it to another room?"

"When we get back to the house we can take another look around, just to be sure, all right?" Instead of answering me, he looked over my head and motioned to someone.

"Hey, Carl. I was about to talk Kate into dessert. Join us?" Carl Caine gave Mike a slight smile, barely nodded to me, and sat down. He accepted a cigarette from Mike who ordered apple pie and coffee for all of us. Caine was a larger man than Mike, filling the space around me, invading it in a way Mike didn't.

"How's business, Carl?"

"The antique business is irrational. As usual." Carl did not meet my eyes directly, but each time I looked up he was watching me, his steady gaze making the blood come to my cheeks.

"Not the antiques, I mean the real business." Mike glanced at me. "Sometime have Carl show you his rooms behind the Pie Safe. He's an artist with furniture."

"I'm doing all right, Mike." He did not give me an invitation. I remembered the sawdust covered hand that had held out a glass of water the day I had my fainting spell. He ate in silence while Mike talked about how Carl had been first in his class at Hawks Crossing High School and had intrigued the girls with his "silent, dark, and handsome ways." The two apparently were good friends who allowed for some ribbing.

Carl's eyes were on my face again when I looked up. I smiled. His chair scraped the floor as he pushed it back. "I'm sorry about Mr. Gerard . . . your grandfather. He was a good man. We'll be at the funeral to pay our respects. Not Sissy, of course, but Mother and me."

I chose to ignore the fact that no smile had answered mine. "Thanks, Carl. I met Sissy this afternoon. Do you think she might come to the house when we get together after the burial? We'll have a small meal."

He hesitated a moment. "I'll ask her. I know she'd like to come, it's just that she isn't comfortable in a crowd."

After he left, Mike and I sat silent for awhile. "You're wondering about Carl." He leaned forward a bit and lowered his voice although there was no one else at the tables around us.

"Carl's mother, Kendra, was Alice Munro's granddaughter. Your grandmother Emily, your great-aunt Maddy, and Kendra used to play in the Munro House when they were children. Kendra Caine has been a widow for many years. After the fire, Carl stayed at home to help his mother care for Sissy. He's devoted to his sister. Carl's a good man and a fine carpenter—an artist with wood."

Mike drove me back to Aunt Jessie's house and without any more conversation, we began a careful search of all the rooms, opening cabinets, reaching to the top of closets and going through the piles of books. We finished in Grandfather's room, searching the Eastlake bureau, the stuffed chair, and the drawer in the bedside table. Mike even looked under the bed. Grandfather's few clothes and two small boxes of papers and photographs were in the tiny closet. Neither box contained a copy of his will. I didn't tell Mike about the small attic room, its door hidden by an old quilt hanging on the wall. I ran my hand over the top of the table, which looked bare without the wedding picture that I had removed from it to place on the casket. When we were finished we walked downstairs. The fireplace in the parlor was empty and I could smell that dank odor of old fires. "It's cooled down, Mike. Let's make a fire to take the chill off the house." We went into the yard beyond the potting shed to the woodpile. There was an ample supply, but I told Mike that Aunt Jessie would need more wood before winter and asked where I could buy some.

"Call Caine farm," Mike said. "One of Carl's men will deliver."

For a moment, I was surprised by the memory of Carl's cold, blue gaze, the feeling of hard hands stopping my fall.

When we laid the fire, I stopped Mike just as he was about to light it. "Will you do something for me now, before it gets dark?" He blew out the match he had just lit and looked at me. He shook his head, "Sure."

"Thanks," I said. "Please take me to the Munro House."

The house was a short drive from Aunt Jessie's. It stood on a small knoll, surrounded by trees. All that remained was a jumble of bricks and the stone hearth. Weeds had grown up around it. "Nothing here now but jimson, butterweed, and wild mustard, Kate." As I walked toward the ruin, Mike caught my hand. "Careful. There's an old well here, under all this brush and debris. The whole area should be fenced off."

"Why hasn't it been?"

"It's because no one comes here, Kate. Ever since the fire, the place has had a strange effect on the locals. For all of that, though, your grandfather refused to sell the land when he had the chance."

"Someone isn't afraid to come here." I walked carefully toward some foxtail growing in a tall clump a few yards away. An empty bottle of beer and a crumpled package of cigarettes were at my feet. It struck me as a desecration, an intentional littering. Anger began to fill my chest. "Let's go, Mike. I've seen enough for now." Suddenly the anger gave way to a deep hurting. I began to cry and his arms drew me against his shoulder. After a while he put his finger under my chin and looked into my eyes with the searching expression I had seen before. "Who are you? Are you as much like your mother as you look or are you the girl I remember?" He brushed my lips quickly with his and we walked back to the car. We made no further mention of the kiss or the question.

The next morning I paid a visit to the Caine farm.

It was after six when I turned onto the long driveway that led to Carl Caine's Italianate, red brick house. A wide porch wrapped around the front and one side. The shutters had been painted recently and purple asters and yellow marigolds bordered the walk. Two carved rocking chairs and a wicker table completed the inviting effect.

"Looking for somebody?" I turned to face the thickset man who had spoken. He stepped back as if I had struck him. "I'm here to buy some firewood for Jessie McCann. My name is Kate Brady. I'm Jessie's niece." I held out my hand but only the air between us received it. "I'm Kyle Krause," he said after a moment's silence. "You have to go to the shed to see about the wood. I'm picking up some myself." He did not offer condolences.

"Are you Opal's son?"

"One of them. I have a brother. He doesn't live here. Decided to join the Air Force, was sent to Japan, and stayed there. Now he has two yellow kids he thinks should call me uncle. You're Elizabeth's girl, right?"

"That's what I'm told," I responded bitterly without thinking. "I've been gone a long time."

"Not surprising when you think of it." I felt as though I'd been struck. He looked at me with half a smile. "Why did you come back? Here to get your inheritance?" The question was sharp and rude.

I flushed with anger. "I didn't even know my grandfather was taken ill until I saw Opal. Anyway, it's none of your business."

"Be surprised what my business may be," he responded

with an unpleasant laugh and walked toward a blue pickup truck carrying a load of firewood.

I decided to get my wood another day. As I turned to go, I caught sight of Sissy's thin face framed in long dark hair, staring at me through the pane of the front door. I waved but the face disappeared.

That night, after a long bath, I put on a nightgown and found Jessie's flannel robe to wrap around me against the coolness of the rooms. Madeleine's journal was on the table in my bedroom. I rested my hand on the book for a moment, relishing my rising excitement at the prospect of continuing my journey into the mind of my great-aunt. When I picked up the book and walked downstairs, I realized with some surprise that I was completely comfortable in the house. Although alone, I was neither lonely nor afraid, especially when I was in Grandfather's room. I pushed that thought out of my mind immediately. It was too strange.

I lit the fire and filled the teapot with water I had set to boiling on the stove. The fireplace filled the small living room with warmth and flickering light. I sat on the sofa, adjusted the lamp on the side table, and found the place where I had stopped reading.

A pounding on the door shook me from Maddy's spell. It was dark and I wasn't expecting anyone but, filled with a sense of well-being, I went to the door. "Who is it?" I asked.

"It's Kyle. Kyle Krause." I hesitated for a moment, and then opened the door. He was leaning against the side of the entryway. His eyes swept over me with the same slow insolence I remembered from our last meeting. He made me angry and I stepped forward to show him I wasn't afraid.

"Yes?" My tone was intentionally even and unfriendly. His response was a laugh and a move forward that caused me to step back rather than touch him.

"No need for you to take that tone with me. Not with me." He laughed again. He stood looking at me with a grin that became a smirk. "Been seeing that lawyer? Any more news about the will? The word's out, you know, that there is no will." He pursed his lips and cocked his head. "Lucky for me."

"What are you talking about?" He came closer, so close I could feel his breath as he looked down at me. It was then, when he was looking down at me, that I remembered. I remembered all of it, all at once. I began to shake and moved back into the room. I sat on the sofa and closed my eyes. I felt him sit next to me and I knew he was remembering all of it, too.

"Just don't get too sure of yourself and what's yours. Sometimes bad things happen to little girls who play with fire, don't they? Never thought you'd be the one to help old Kyle. Never did get a chance to thank you." I opened my eyes and he laughed at the shock on my face.

"What do you mean?" My heart was pounding and I could not control an involuntary shudder.

"Now, girl, you remember the day I found you sleeping in the shed. Twenty years ago, sure, but you remember." And as his hateful voice droned on, slowly and with relish he relived every detail of that day for me. It was happening again.

"Well, Kate, it's like this. You'd better get ready to share with me. I'm your own uncle, girl, well your half-uncle, on the wrong side of the blanket if you get my meaning."

He reached down and pulled me against him, his mouth coming down hard on mine, his tongue forcing itself against my teeth. He had a sour smell. When he let me go I wiped my mouth with my hand and stared at him. The fear had drained away and I felt cold and numb. Something told me how to play his game.

"That needs some practice," I said, coldly. His face flushed and the grin faded. He raised his hand to hit me but dropped it before my unflinching stare. He sat absolutely motionless for a moment except for the clenching and unclenching of his fists. Finally he spoke in a hoarse whisper, "You'll be sorry for that." He stood up and gave me a look that made my skin prickle with fear. He left me without another word. I watched him leave, then closed and locked the door. I pushed away the old memory that threatened to return by remembering his kiss. It was meant to disgust and threaten me enough to chase me away. It wouldn't work. What he had done was confuse me further. Why had he hated Elizabeth, my mother? I wondered. And why did he call himself my uncle?

I was sitting across from the O'dell watercolor, waiting for Mike to return. I could not believe that Kyle was my grandfather's son. I wanted Mike to tell me how to fight the preposterous claim. I heard his footsteps in the hall and stood up as he entered the room.

"Sorry to make you wait, Kate, but I was in court." I followed him into his office. "I got your message, and I got something else, as well. This was on my secretary's desk this morning." He handed me an envelope.

He watched me as I read the copy of a letter written by my grandfather to Opal Krause, telling her that he believed her claim that Kyle was his son from his intimacies with her before his marriage. He said he would help her with the expense of raising the boy but that he did not want her to tell Gene, as that would destroy their lifelong friendship. He said if she told Emily, he would deny the whole situation.

"What does this mean, Mike?"

"In the absence of a will, the State of Indiana will distribute your grandfather's estate to his surviving children or their issue. This letter, if it is genuine, would give Kyle equal rights of inheritance with Jessie and with you as Elizabeth's only remaining child."

"Mike, if my grandfather left him out of his will and he knew it, he would have had to destroy the will or he wouldn't inherit anything, would he?"

"That's true, Kate, but is there any reason to think he did that?"

"He despises me, Mike. If he had to destroy the will to inherit, I'm sure he would do it. I feel his anger every time he looks at me and . . . " I stopped short of telling Mike about the kiss. It was too disgusting. I blurted out the ugly suspicion that came unbidden into my thoughts. "Mike, I think he could have caused that fire at the hospital."

"That's a dangerous thought, Kate. Why not just let things rest until after the funeral. I'll have to question him about this letter and then we'll see about any part he had in the fire."

I left Mike's office and decided to stop at the coffee shop for a sandwich. When I pushed the glass door open, I saw Carl Caine sitting at a table in the back of the room. He looked up as I entered and stood up slowly, motioning me to join him. I hesitated a moment, but gave in to a growing curiosity to know him better. That curiosity surprised me, even worried me a little. I hadn't wanted to know all about a man since Drew. I ordered coffee and a hamburger and wondered what to say.

"Mike says you need some firewood. If you'll tell me where you want it, I'll deliver it." His blue eyes touched mine for just a moment.

"Thanks. Just leave it at the side porch." For a moment the memory of Sissy's face came to me. "How's Sissy? I hoped she might come out of the house and say hello." I stopped. How foolish I sounded because Sissy didn't say "hello" or anything else.

Carl saw my discomfort and smiled. The smile was slow and devastating. "Sissy is very shy. If anyone could get her to come out of her shell though, it would be you." He stopped smiling, bent his head and studied his hands. "You remind her of Elizabeth."

"I remind you of Elizabeth, too." I heard myself saying.

"What was she like?" He didn't answer and he didn't look up. Then he took a deep breath like someone preparing to face a difficult task. Each word seemed to be wrung from him, with long pauses between as if he needed to gather strength for what he had to say.

"She wasn't like anybody else. Elizabeth had a strangeness about her, a kind of excitement. She made flowers grow in poor earth and she could whistle a hawk from the sky. She smiled a great deal and never worried at all." His words grew softer. "I thought she was the most beautiful woman I ever saw. I used to watch the house sometimes just to get a glimpse of her. I'll never forget the night I was bringing over some wood and saw her dancing with Terry on the porch. She was wearing a long white dress and her hair was loose on her shoulders. In the moonlight she looked unreal. Just an adolescent's crush, but I still remember hearing the music and watching them dance." His eyes caught mine suddenly. "And, yes, you remind me of her." He looked at me directly for the first time. "Why do you call her Elizabeth instead of Mother?"

"Because she was unreal in my life. Any early memories I had have faded. She's just a photo in an old album. She never mothered me. I know she's my mother only because I've been told so and because I resemble her."

For one painful moment I hated myself for changing the color of my hair. I wanted him to see the real me. I wanted to tell him that the dark color was a sham. But I needed to keep my strong resemblance to my mother. At least until I paid certain people back for what they had done to me. No, not certain people. Just one person now. Just Aunt Jessie. And I admitted to myself for the first time, that I found myself ashamed of wanting to hurt her that way.

The waitress came to the table with my food and refilled Carl's coffee cup. I stared at the hamburger on my plate. The slice of tomato was thick and as red as in the poster on the wall. I needed to say something. "Do you think Sissy would come to the house and sit with me after the funeral tomorrow? I'd appreciate the company."

"I think she would like that. I'll ask her."

As I walked to the wooden steps in front of the frame church, Carl Caine and his mother joined me. Carl's face was strained above his dark suit. Mrs. Caine lowered her eyes. "I'm sorry he's dead. Edward was a good man." I didn't want to argue that, so I simply nodded my head and turned to Carl with a question in my eyes.

"I'm sorry but Sissy isn't coming. She hasn't been inside a church since the fire. After the fire at the hospital, I guess it all came back to her. She's refused to leave the house at all. When I told her we were burying your grandfather, she cried. She'll probably come to the cemetery later by herself. She barely sleeps now and she cries a lot. It's not as bad as the first time, but it's bad." He looked down to hide the look in his eyes. As they walked away from me, I wondered again what Sissy had seen the day of the fire.

The homily was all about surviving tragedy and the mysteries of our brief lives. Only love and trust are demanded of us, Fr. James said. Only love and trust can bring meaning to the strange paths we sometimes walk. As I watched people return from receiving communion, I noticed Mike in the line. He smiled and moved into the pew behind me. I turned and saw that Opal sat alone. I wasn't surprised that Kyle had not come. A few older men and women I did not know spoke to me after Mass. One of them was Sally Stonebreaker, who had kept house for Alice Munro and who knew Edward and his family when the girls were children. She told me that Alice often spoke of the day they buried my grandmother, Emily Gerard. Her death broke the older woman's heart. She said the day of the burial was the saddest she could remember. "They loosed Emily's hawk that day, you know. It was like seeing her soul fly free, Miz Munro said. Edward got very close with his girls after that and they kept to themselves. Used to be that Opal's son Kyle had been helping out, but after they buried Emily he didn't come around no more and the families didn't seem so close."

As I stood alone at my grandfather's grave, I was filled with a sudden fierce curiosity about where Elizabeth and Terry were buried. I walked to a bench under a honey locust tree and sat for a few minutes to sort out my feelings before beginning to look for their graves. I was exhausted and closed my eyes. Sleep deprived and emotionally exhausted, I slept. It was getting dark when Carl's voice woke me.

"Kate, have you seen Sissy? I thought she might come here after everyone left." He was clearly worried. "I thought she might come here to be with you. She often comes to Elizabeth's grave." I was fully awake because of my concern for Sissy.

"Let me help you look for her, Carl."

He frowned. "You may not want to, Kate, because the other place I've found her is the Munro House." The way he said my name, hesitating a bit first, gave me a strange feeling in my stomach.

We didn't find Sissy. He dropped me off where Jessie's driveway met the road and drove on to his house to see if she had returned.

I was startled to see that the front door was open. Sissy was standing just inside, her long hair as dark as the eyes she raised to mine. She put her arms around me and we held each other for a moment before we went into the house. It was cold, so I moved to start the fire that I had laid before leaving that morning. The dry wood caught easily, crackling around the small pieces of kindling. Sissy stood in the farthest corner of the room, wrapping her arms around herself, her face white and frightened.

"I'm sorry, Sissy, but we need the heat. Don't be afraid—the fire is safe in the hearth. Sit here, please, while I call your brother. Carl's been looking for you." I could hear the relief in

Carl's voice when I told him his sister was with me. I promised I'd drive Sissy home later and hung up.

She sat in the old rocker after she had pushed it farther from the flames. They cast a flickering light on the beautiful carvings on the back and arms of the rocker. Following my eyes, she smiled and ran her small fingers along the carvings. She held out her arm and I saw a wooden bracelet carved with the same style of flowers and unicorns. She took a comb from her hair and showed me another lovely example of the carver's work. I wondered if it was possible that she had created this beauty. "Did you do this, Sissy?"

She shook her head and looked at me. Of course. I recalled Mike's conversation with Carl at the snack shop. "These are Carl's work, aren't they?" She smiled. I remembered the carved desk in Mike's office. Carl was a talented man.

I fixed some cheese sandwiches and tea and put them on the table in front of the sofa. Because of the lack of conversation, I turned on the phonograph. She came over eagerly and sat on the floor as I went through the stack of records. I chose the Chopin polonaises and remembered the waltz I had heard in the Pie Safe the day I fainted in Carl's shop. She sat back in the rocker and closed her eyes as the music filled the room. Lost in our own thoughts, we spent the evening after my grandfather's funeral comforting each other through this quiet listening.

I don't know how many records we listened to or just how much time passed before she got up and hugged me. I was startled when she pulled away. She looked up at the mantle clock and almost ran across the room. I caught her at the door and told her I would drive her home. That earned me another warm hug. When we reached the house Carl was sitting on the porch swing. He smiled at me for the first time I could remember, a smile that went almost all the way to his eyes. My heart beat harder and faster and something happened to the pit of my stomach. Sissy jumped out of the car, kissed his cheek, and hurried into the house.

I got out of the car and stood looking up at Carl. "Sissy was suddenly in a big hurry to get home so she let me drive her back." I realized that I was smiling. Sissy was the one bright spot in my life.

"Yes." He glanced up and I heard the sound of shutters closing. "Ever since the fire in the hospital she closes her windows early every evening and stays in her room for the rest of the night. I'm glad she came to see you. Maybe now she'll begin to come back to life again." He stopped the swing and faced me squarely. "Kate, will you go to dinner with me tonight?" I was surprised. At the offer and at my response. I smiled again. "Thanks, Carl. I'd like that." I felt warmth rising in my cheeks and almost hoped he noticed. "Let me go home and change. Pick me up in half an hour."

I was considering wearing my blue shirtwaist when I walked quickly up the steps. There was a package outside my door. I tore off the paper and my hands curled around the scorched fur of a bedraggled teddy bear. My fear was so great that for a moment I couldn't breathe. I sat on the steps and stared at it. When I could move again, I went to the barn, pulled out a shovel, and buried the thing.

The Vietnamese restaurant Carl took me to was a short drive out of town in an old clapboard house that was painted yellow. There were tables on the lawn but no one else was having dinner yet. I hadn't decided whether to say anything to Carl about what Kyle had told me and about the teddy bear. A small, thin man came to our table as we seated ourselves. "Hello, Mr. Caine." He smiled at Carl but his smile faded when he looked at me. He left us abruptly. Carl excused himself to follow the man into the restaurant. I began to perspire and I felt a heaviness in my chest. Something was very wrong. When Carl reappeared, a tiny woman wearing Vietnamese dress was with him.

She gave me a distracted bow and then she and Carl sat down. The woman was the wife of the owner who had left us in such haste. She spoke in heavily accented English. Her dark eyes held mine as she said that her husband had been badly frightened by a man he had met years earlier when the Vietnamese couple first settled in Hawks Crossing. A large man had followed them to the parking lot of the grocery store one evening. He was visibly angry and about to strike her husband, shouting things the Vietnamese had not understood. It was because the woman who was with the frightening man intervened that her husband had not been hurt. "My husband said you are the woman who saved him. But that cannot be because it happened many years ago and you have not aged. He was frightened that you are a strange spirit who has come to take his soul in payment for your help."

My startling resemblance to the woman who saved him had terrified the man! My resemblance to Elizabeth. Carl explained that I was the daughter of that woman and no bad spirit. He asked her to explain this to her husband. She inclined her head to both of us and left the table.

We walked for awhile after leaving the restaurant. I was lost in my effort to understand what I had heard, lost in this latest glimpse into the life of my parents. Carl took my arm and tentatively drew me closer to him. It seemed to help, but by the time we reached his car, I had begun to cry. Suddenly I was telling him about the thing I had buried and what Kyle had told me. "It's all right, Kate." He unlocked the car door and then put his arms around me in comfort. For a moment, after he pulled away and looked into my face, I was certain he was going to say something. Instead he bent to kiss me. His mouth was full and the kiss filled the empty spaces inside me. He felt my response.

After I got in, he closed the door, walked around the car to settle behind the steering wheel, and reached for me. He began to kiss me again but I put my hand against his chest to push him away.

"It's not me you're kissing, you're kissing Elizabeth. I'm

not Elizabeth, I'm Kate. And I'll tell you something else. I've dyed my hair darker to make all of you think I look like her. My hair is blonde. I'm not Elizabeth."

His low laugh answered me.

"No, thank God, you're not. She was a boy's first dream. You're the reality. Elizabeth wasn't afraid of anything, and the only person she ever needed was Terry. All you want from me is comfort now, but give me some time. Let me prove it's you who attracts me. Take the time to know me. Please. And get rid of the dye job as soon as possible. I want to see the real color of your hair." His mouth was soft and I felt myself responding to kisses even more convincing than his words. I knew that I wanted to believe him.

By the time he took me home, I wasn't crying anymore. But I was bemused. I had never cared for anybody but Drew and suddenly there were two men in my life and I was drawn to both of them.

Sissy came to visit me every day that week. We stayed in Jessie's house, listening to music and sometimes playing cards. She didn't object when I lit a fire toward evening and she even sat a bit closer to the fireplace. When I got up to drive her home, she shook her head. She stood on the porch, looked in the direction of her home, and made a running motion with her hand.

"Well, Sissy, a little exercise is probably what you need. Come tomorrow. Please." An idea came to me. "Wait, Sissy, I have something for you."

I ran upstairs to get the locket I had placed in the drawer of the bedside table. As I looked at it lying in my hand, I knew it was meant for Sissy. I walked quickly down the stairs and held it out to her.

There was no way for me to prepare for her reaction to the gift. Her face went gray and she stood absolutely still. When she looked at me again, her eyes were hopeful. Her lips moved as she tried to speak. "Baby?" she whispered. She held up the locket and smiled. "Baby?" She kissed her fingertips and touched the small silver cross she was wearing. Then she turned and ran down the stairs. I watched her go, wondering if she had really spoken or if I had imagined it.

About seven, the telephone rang. It was Carl's voice and he sounded concerned. Sissy hadn't come home. I told him what time she had left and that she had been in a surprisingly happy mood. I asked what I could do to help. He said he was going to look for her and asked me to keep an eye out for her. I didn't tell him that Sissy had spoken. Let him find out for himself, I thought and found myself smiling.

As I hung up, I heard Mike's car. He came in and as I was telling Mike about the call I realized that, despite Sissy's happy mood, I was worried about her. He reminded me that Sissy often would disappear for an hour or two and that Carl always found her. We decided to go on to dinner at a home-style restaurant Mike liked. Driving to Tyler's, my thoughts kept going back to the shocked expression on the face of the Vietnamese man a week ago. When I looked up, we were passing near the ruins of the Munro House.

"Let's take a look, Mike. I can't explain it but I think perhaps she went to the house tonight." He started to object but changed his mind and we drove directly there. Leaving the car in the overgrown driveway, we walked around the building. As we moved toward the location of the old well, Mike reminded me to be careful. I looked up and noticed a large gap in the weeds. I called to Mike and he moved carefully into the area and looked down. The expression on his face tightened. "She's here, Kate. She's fallen into the well."

An hour later Dr. Reuter told us that Sissy was dead. Carl held his mother in his arms. She moaned softly and closed her eyes as she leaned against him. Carl's grief was frightening because it was silent. I wanted to comfort him but I knew he had withdrawn to a place I couldn't reach, and so I lost myself in my own deep misery. I had come to love Sissy and to hope that through our growing friendship she would regain her speech. Now that sweet friendship was beyond me and her words would be spoken in another world.

That night Mike took me home and stayed with me until I fell asleep. He told me that he had not found the missing will and we had 30 days to produce it before the State of Indiana determined how Edward Gerard's estate would be probated. He put his arms around me before he left and placed his cheek against mine. I leaned against him, grateful for his warmth. I told him I would call him tomorrow.

The morning we assembled in Mike's office to learn the conditions of probate under the laws of Indiana, Kyle and Opal arrived before I did. Kyle looked at me with barely concealed triumph. His mother looked neither at Kyle nor at me while Mike explained that the house, investments, business ownership, and bank accounts would be distributed equally among Jessie, if she survived, myself as Elizabeth's heir and Kyle, as Edward Gerard's acknowledged illegitimate son. An inventory was yet incomplete. There was silence until Opal spoke.

"It's right. My Kyle is Eddie's son. She couldn't give him sons." She turned to look at me directly. "Your mother was nothing to be proud of. Married that crazy drunk that burned down the best house in the county and took the reason from poor Sissy. Why did you come back? You made her think of Elizabeth and go back to the house. She'd be alive except for . . . "

"Mrs. Krause!" Mike interrupted.

"Leave Ma alone, Mike. She's right." Kyle's eyes glared at me.

Those eyes burned with hatred. "You shouldn't have any of it. You brought the trouble here. Just everyone won't believe it. You're not wanted, never have been." Mike saw the look on my face and ended the meeting. He said he would get in touch with each of us. I left as quickly as possible. Wanting to talk to Carl, I decided to go to the Pie Safe.

The bell jangled as I opened the door, but neither Carl nor his mother came into the shop. I walked to the back room and called to him over the sound of a recording of baroque music. He came at once, his hands filled with a box of books. The look on my face made him put the books down, walk close to me, and put his hands on my shoulders.

He pulled me closer and I found the comfort I needed in those blue eyes and his strong body. I leaned against him, my arms tightening around him. When he kissed me and held me closer, I relaxed and told him about the meeting.

"Kyle is a strange, frightening man. I always found it hard to believe that he and Greg are brothers. But then, Gene practically raised Greg by himself. Opal only had time for Kyle." He looked at me with a small smile. "Kate, I've wanted to hold you like this since the first time I saw you. At least I can be grateful to Kyle for making you so unhappy that you came to me."

I pushed away slightly and let the ugly thought surface. "Was it me you wanted to hold or did you want to pretend I'm my mother?"

He moved away from me and fingered some of my long, dark hair. "It's true, I did love her and you looked so much like her the day you came into the store that I couldn't believe it. But it's you I'm falling in love with." His eyes were holding mine in a sad, probing look.

I wanted him to hold me and to make me believe him. But I didn't touch him again. This wasn't the time.

"Come to my house later and I'll fix some dinner and we'll talk all this out," I said.

On my way home, I felt the need to go back to the ruins, but as I drove toward the house, I had a strong feeling that I should go to the hospital. Trusting my instincts, I drove there directly.

When I got to the nurses' station, I was greeted with a

smile. "Your Aunt Jessie seems better today. Perhaps, if you go in now you can have a few good words with her."

This time when I came into the room, the face on the pillow smiled at me. Aunt Jessie held up her hand and called me.

"Oh, Katie, it is you. Dear God, how much you look like her!" She stared at me in silence then shook her head as if to clear it. "They said you've been visiting me every day. Please come here and give me a kiss. I've missed you, child, more than you can ever know and I have mourned the way time and my illness cheated us from knowing each other well." The weight in my chest began to shatter and I felt light. Her words drove my anger into a corner of my heart. I wanted to laugh and to cry and to run to tell someone the news that I was missed and that I was loved. "Aunt Jessie, I'm so glad that you're better." She wanted to know about me—everything I could tell her quickly. She did not ask about Grandfather, so I knew she was not remembering everything that had happened. She did seem to remember part of it.

"Kate, did you hear about the fire? They had to move me because it started in my room. It must have happened after Kyle left. I was so exhausted by our argument that I fell asleep. He is a terrible man. I wasn't up to arguing with him." Her expression became puzzled and then tired and drained.

"What did he argue with you about?

"He told me Mike Collier sent him to ask me about my father's will. He wanted Kyle to go to the house and pick it up. Something about the need to update it now that I'm not well. Kyle said your Grandpa gave him the executor's powers and he wanted to replace the old will with a new one. Well, that didn't sound right so I told him to go to Mike for help. But he got so angry that he frightened me and I finally decided it didn't matter and I told him it was in the bookcase downstairs. Was that all right?" Her eyes closed as though the long speech had exhausted her small supply of energy.

It took me a moment to gain control of my anger, but

when I spoke my voice was calm. "It was all right, Aunt Jessie, you did just fine. Soon you'll be well enough to come home and then we can have a nice long visit. I'll be back soon." As I turned to go, I heard her voice, again, a bit distant and soft. "Elizabeth? I took care of her, dear. I took care of her." The hope that had risen in me fled at the sound of her words.

I left the hospital and drove back to Mike's office but his secretary told me that he had gone to Indianapolis and would not return until the next afternoon. I would have to wait to tell him about the will.

On the way home, I stopped at the store and picked up some pork chops, fresh green beans, and new potatoes. For the moment I put aside the questions Aunt Jessie's words had raised in my mind. Instead I began to concentrate on my disturbing relationship with Carl.

I had just finished mixing the salad for our dinner, when I heard a knock at the door. "Come in, Carl," I called. The knocking continued. I walked to the door and opened it to see the tense, young nurse I had met outside Aunt Jessie's room.

"Good evening, Miss Gerard. I'm Donna Wilson. Sorry to disturb you, but I had to talk to you."

"Come in." I wiped my hands on the dishcloth I had carried to the door and invited her to sit on the sofa.

"No, thank you. I just have something I think belongs to you." She held out her hand. The locket I had given Sissy gleamed on her palm. I took it and looked at her curiously. "Where did you find it?" She seemed very uncomfortable.

"You have to understand, Miss Brady, that Kyle sometimes does things without thinking them through. It fell out of the pocket of his jacket when he left my house last night. I picked it up thinking it was mine. He means no harm, but I knew it was yours because I had seen you wearing it at the hospital."

The gold locket seemed to burn in my hand. I looked at it as though I had never seen it before. But now I knew I had. Not just when I bought it at the Pie Safe. I had known it much longer.

With stunned certainty I knew that it was the mate to great-uncle Fredryk's watch fob that Delores rubbed between her fingers like an amulet. I was sure now that his locket held a miniature of my great-aunt Madeleine. What had this locket held?

"Where did he get it?"

She looked at me directly. "I don't know. I only know he took what wasn't his and I'm returning it. Please try to forgive him. He doesn't really mean any harm. We're . . . well we're planning to get married soon and I don't want anything to spoil that."

Before I could think of a response, she left. I told Carl about it when he arrived.

"It's strange, Carl, but my Uncle Fredryk had a gold locket on his watch chain and it matches this one. He gave it to his daughter Delores. It must have belonged to my great-aunt Maddy. I'm sure now that his has a picture of her inside. I wonder why there was no picture in this one.

"I don't know, Kate. That locket probably came to us from an estate. There was no picture in it." We looked at each other in silence. We had just begun dinner when Kendra called, telling Carl she had been having chest pains and asking him to come home. "I'm sorry, Kate, but I'll have to go. She sounds very anxious."

As his car pulled out of the driveway, I surrendered to my growing suspicion that Kendra was less anxious about her heart than about Carl's relationship with me. I had felt her dislike since the first day I saw her at the Pie Safe.

The next morning when I dressed for the day, I wore the locket. I decided to stop at the flower shop near the hospital before visiting Jessie. As I got out of the car, I saw Kyle walking toward me.

He stood absolutely still. "Where did you get that? He was pointing at my locket. I had the overwhelming desire to anger him.

"Why I found it. Can you imagine where?" I was certain that his thoughts were racing.

"Don't make too much of that bit of gold. It doesn't prove anything except that you had better be careful." He was trying to control himself.

"How did you happen to 'find' it, Kyle? Did you frighten poor Sissy into giving it to you? Did you bully her? Did you . . ." My mind revolted at the thought that consumed me but I continued. "Did you push her?"

He looked at me for a long time in silence.

"Why did you push her?"

"Why would you imagine that I would do such a thing? Why would I want to hurt that poor fool?"

I took a shot in the dark. "Probably because she saw you start the fire in Aunt Jessie's room after you argued with the poor old woman. She couldn't tell on you, Kyle, so why did you have to kill her? She was already silent."

His face was dark with his rising rage. "No she wasn't. She could speak some words again. So she told you. I thought so. I followed her from your house to the ruin. When she saw me she said "Fire," and started to run. Not fast enough.

I was shaking. "You admit it," I said.

"Not hardly," he answered in a more normal tone. There's no one but the two of us who know Sissy could talk and you are only guessing that I killed her. There's no proof and I'll swear I never said any of this. Try to prove something, make any trouble at all and what happened to her will happen to you." I was about to tell Kyle what Donna had told me but some inner voice told me to keep that knowledge to myself. I was silent as he pushed me aside and walked past me.

I walked to Mike's office through the fog of my own confused thoughts, not noticing the shops I passed or the people around me. As quickly as I could I told Mike all that Kyle said to me and I told him what Aunt Jessie had said about Kyle's visit and the will. I was afraid to tell Carl, afraid he might do something drastic to avenge his sister.

"I'll find Kyle and talk to him," Mike said, his face more worried than angry. Mike made the call and Opal answered and said that Kyle wasn't at home, but that Mike was welcome to come to the house. Mike said he wanted to talk to Opal alone about her son and that he would call me later. In the meantime, he suggested that I visit Aunt Jessie as I had planned.

I was confused and sick with apprehension but I knew I couldn't help Mike so I decided to go to the hospital.

I bought some yellow roses and a few stems of Queen Anne's Lace wrapped in thin green tissue. When I entered Aunt Jessie's room, I prayed she would be alert. She seemed very weak but she took the bouquet with pleasure and her greeting came from a clear mind.

"Come here, Katie. Oh, my dear child, how I wanted you to get to know your grandfather and me. Forgive us for sending you away after the fire."

She held out her arms. I felt the last of my suspicions fall away and I put my arms around her.

"At first everyone believed that Terry had caused the fire but then Kyle started to spread his awful story. Some people believed it and I was too confused and ill to fight it."

I looked into her face and saw my worst fears reflected there. "Tell me, Aunt Jessie. It's all right." My heart was beating fast and hard in terror of what she would say.

"He said . . . that awful man said . . . that he had caught you playing with matches the week before the fire. He said that he found you in a corner of the potting shed. He said . . . he said you had set fire to your teddy bear and he stopped you for fear you'd burn yourself and burn down the shed as well." Her eyes were streaming as she brought her face close to mine. "I didn't believe it then and I don't believe it now. But how could I protect you? The county sheriff talked to you and he said you cried and cried and said your teddy bear was dead and then you became hysterical. Even the sheriff was wondering about you. I was on the verge of a nervous breakdown and your grandfather had to be sent to a nursing home to recuperate. We couldn't keep you. Your great-aunt Madeleine had a daughter in Chicago, and I thought your life would be easier there. And there wouldn't be any terrible talk that you would have to face growing up here."

My mind was playing competing messages. I kept hearing her say I had set fire to my teddy bear. But there was a strange roaring in my head as I heard a little girl's voice shouting, "No, don't do it, don't do it." I took a deep breath and realized my aunt was talking again.

"But, there is something else I have to tell you, now, in case I slip away again. The night of the fire, Sissy rushed into my house and found me asleep on the rocker. I had been dreaming that Elizabeth came into the room. I woke up to feel Sissy tugging at my arm. Her eyes were wide and dilated and she was crying hysterically. For a moment I did not see the small bundle she held tightly in her right arm. Half asleep, I seemed to hear Elizabeth's voice, 'Promise me, promise me,' and I hallucinated that Elizabeth was in front of me carrying a small infant wrapped in a pink blanket. Through her sobs, Sissy started to tell me about the fire. I heard Ben shouting for me. In my waking dream, I took the child from Sissy who was shaking with fright, and put the tiny creature into the white bassinet I had placed in our room for the day Elizabeth would bring her child to visit us. Your grandfather was living with us at the time and he stumbled down the stairs when he heard the shouting. Father and I joined Ben on the porch and we ran to help.

After the fire and when I knew they all were dead, that Ben and Elizabeth and the baby were dead, I lost all sense of myself. I vaguely remember that my father and I were holding each other tightly and crying like we would never stop. Then I lost consciousness.

"What about the other baby?" I asked.

Jessie wept as though her heart were bursting. "Katie, I

suffered so much and for no reason. It was all a dream. A strange and awful dream. But I didn't know that. For a long time I was hysterical and kept demanding that the baby be brought to me."

I stroked her hair and asked, "Did they look for the baby?" She began to shake her head over and over.

"There was no baby. Just the little one that died in the fire. They said I dreamed the second baby while under the influence of the drugs they gave me to calm me."

"Hush, Aunt Jessie." My face was wet with tears, for Jessie, for me, for Sissy, for the little baby who had died in the fire and for the little baby who had been in my aunt's agonizing dream. The rest of the tears were for fear that Aunt Jessie was wrong, and that I had set the fire. The weight of that horror crushed me. Kyle was an evil man but he could have been right. I might have had a fascination with fire that even his awful tormenting hadn't stopped. Aunt Jessie didn't know that. She kept talking.

"Even now, I'm haunted by a dream of Elizabeth coming to me, asking me where her baby is. I tell her the baby is safe but she keeps asking me, 'Where is my baby?' over and over. It's so real. I try to comfort her. I tell her I took care of the baby and then she goes away. But the dream always comes back. It's so hard, Katie. Sometimes I'm afraid to go to sleep." The strain of telling me about the dream tired Aunt Jessie. She cried softly for awhile in my arms. Then she slept.

All the way to Mike's office, my mind swirled with the images of Aunt Jessie's story.

Donna was standing in the hall outside his door when I got there. Her face was swollen and bruised. "Come with me, Miss Brady," she said, as she proceeded to lead me outside.

"Mrs. Krause and Mike were talking when Kyle and I went to pick up my firewood a little bit ago. As soon as he saw Mike, Kyle started yelling at his mother for talking to him. He told her that you and Mike would lie about anything to prevent him from claiming his inheritance. Kyle said that she was the one who had made him a bastard and that everything that had happened was on her head. Then, when he was faced with your statement to Mike and learned that I had given you the locket, he hit me and ran out of the house. We were afraid he would come after you so I drove up here in the hopes of finding you before he got to you."

She had driven Mike's car. We took it back to the house. When we got there Opal was standing beside Mike and for the first time in my life, I pitied her for her pain and helplessness. Donna went to her and held her tightly.

"I've called the police," Mike said.

I felt enormously tired and empty. "I want to go home, Mike, please."

Mike told Donna to call us after the police arrived, and then we drove to Jessie's house. As we approached it, we saw a figure with a torch setting fire to the barn. Kyle looked up, saw the car approaching and ran into the house, setting fire to the rooms. He didn't come out.

I watched the house burning and it was as though some piece of me was being destroyed. I felt suffocated by the billows of smoke, by the loss of so much that was mine. Now I was sure that all the answers to my questions were destroyed, as lost as Madeleine's journal was lost. Mike put his arms around me to stop the shaking I couldn't control. Then he ran from the car to the house, but it wasn't possible to for him to enter. The heat was too great. I knew that Kyle was dead. We drove back to Opal's house.

As we parked the car, Opal and Donna came out on the porch. Opal moved toward me as my knees gave way. She held me against her, supporting my weight with her stronger leg. Then she wrapped me in a throw that lay across the back of a porch chair and she and Donna lowered me into it. Her hands were surprisingly gentle as she chafed my face and arms. When

I opened my eyes, she asked me what had happened. Looking up into her face, emptied of any emotion but concern, I told her about the fire. I couldn't bring myself to tell her about Kyle. Somehow she guessed.

"Oh, Kyle," she said and dropped her head. Donna and Mike leaned over me. Donna's bruised face was shiny with tears that she didn't bother to brush away. Opal reached out for her and they cried in each other's arms. "I'm so sorry," Donna kept saying. Opal didn't answer but let the girl put her arm around her and walk with her to the bedroom. I was feeling better and followed them in case I could help. Opal sat on the bed and then stretched out as though desperately weary. Donna took a crocheted throw from the chair beside the bed and covered her. I noticed that Opal had a small picture in her hand. She studied it for a long while, and then closed her eyes. She turned on her side and the hand with the picture slid under her pillow. I left the bedroom.

Much later Donna came out. She said that Opal had wakened and that when she leaned over her, the old woman had handed her the photo. Donna said she glanced at the baby picture and felt her heart break. She had told Opal that she had tried to get Kyle to accept counseling and medication to deal with his depression and his temper but that he had refused. Donna had asked her to forget what he had said to her and to remember him when he was her little baby. Opal had looked at the picture and then at Donna and had smiled in a way that made her look very young. "Kyle's home now," she said. "God understands better than we do. He's at peace now." She said that she did often think of that little baby and kissed his face before she went to bed each night. Donna held out the picture.

I looked at the faded photo and then turned it over. The name on the back of the picture was Greg.

"But I thought she never paid attention to Greg. It doesn't make sense." I said.

"Maybe it does," Mike smiled at the small face. "Maybe

she couldn't allow herself to show him the love she felt. She had stolen Kyle's right to know his real father and she had to concentrate on making that up to Kyle until she found the way to tell Edward and the boy the truth."

"But it's monstrous, to rob one of her sons of affection in the name of guilt."

"Don't forget that she knew her husband very well, Kate. She knew that Gene would love him enough for both of them. Greg certainly learned his father's peaceful ways, something Opal could never teach him. She only cheated herself, Kate. I'll get word to Greg. He'll come back. Opal needs his love and forgiveness and I believe he'll give it to her. I found some letters in my father's personal files that prove that Gene knew all along that Kyle was not his son. He saw the resemblance to Edward, even though Opal insisted that Kyle looked just like Gene had as a young boy. Gene was a good man. Like father, like son."

The weariness I felt draining me must have shown in my face. Mike pulled me into his arms. "Come on, you. You're spending tonight at my place." I was too weak to argue the amenities of convention, and too grateful. He glanced at me in amusement.

"I live in an old house converted to a double. Sally Stonebreaker lives on the other side. I'll ask her to spend the night with you in my part of the house and your reputation will remain intact. One of the bedrooms has twin beds. You'll be comfortable and have company." As he opened the door to his car, I continued to ask the questions that filled my head as maddeningly as tinnitus.

"If it is really possible for Greg to love his mother after all she's done to him, that's a reason to hope for everything." But was everything forgivable?

"I believe it's possible to love someone beyond reason. Don't you?" Mike slid behind the wheel and reached over for me. He bent down and his kiss was warm and confidently seductive. I felt the need to cling to him, but thought, Is it only because

I need to feel safe and loved right now? I pulled away and smiled at him. "Thanks, kind sir, but what I need right now is some serious sleep."

Inside the gabled white house with its commodious porch and beveled fanlight over the front doors, I found the haven I needed. Mike and Sally fussed over me. The next thing I knew, I was sitting at the oak table in the kitchen taking a sip of a sweet-smelling herbal tea. After seeing me safely settled, Mike returned to Jessie's house. I was too weak and too unhappy to move. My thoughts kept running back to the rooms where my life was in flames. I felt an overwhelming fatigue and began to sob. Sally helped me to the sofa where I rested against a soft cushion and closed my eyes. I must have dozed off because when I opened my eyes I felt better. I began to look around the room and almost at once noticed a small painting that held my eyes with quiet insistence. A man sat in a clearing beside a stream, staring fixedly into a fire. Behind him was a rough cabin fronted with a small porch. There was the suggestion of a woman's figure in the light pouring through an open door onto the porch. I was studying the picture when I finally slipped again into sleep.

I wakened to the sound of someone crying. It took me a moment to realize that I was the source of the heartbreaking sound. Sally must have gone to sleep. I pushed aside the soft throw covering my legs. As the memory of what had happened exploded in my mind, Mike's key turned in the lock.

The smell of acrid smoke from his clothes entered the room before he did. When he saw me, he smiled. "Not asleep? Let me get showered and we'll talk a little, all right?" I nodded and he walked upstairs slowly, each step heavy with fatigue. I walked into the kitchen, found a brown can of Yuban coffee and plugged in his automatic coffee maker.

When he came down, I was sitting at the table holding a

steaming mug. He poured a cup and sat down opposite me. "The fire is out, Kate, but the house is badly damaged."

"What about Kyle?"

"Dead. They recovered the body. And Kate," he reached out and ran a finger along the back of my hand. "They know he set the fire. A couple of kids saw him bring gasoline cans into the house just before they saw the flames. They ran to get the sheriff but when they heard the fire truck going to the house they came back and told the firemen what they had seen."

I sighed but the knot in my stomach remained. Kyle was dead but his death didn't change the fact that I still couldn't be sure I hadn't started the fire that killed my parents.

Maybe after he made me burn my toy, I believed that I was a bad child and set fire to the house. Maybe that was why I had my recurring nightmare.

Mike stood up and took his cup to the sink. Then he turned toward me and held out his arms. He held me for a long time while the floodgates opened and all my anguish poured out. After I quieted somewhat and my breathing became less torn, he kissed my cheeks and my neck. He pushed back the hair that had fallen over my face and then his lips brushed my wet eyes. I pushed him away so I could look into his face. I saw tenderness and a kind of hunger. I answered that look, my mouth pressed against his, my arms tightening around his neck. When he touched me the pain inside me seemed to dull. "Kate," he said, his voice husky and low. "I think I love you very much."

His words hit me like a fist. Drew had said that to me once. I stiffened and pulled away.

"That bad, huh?" His hands went around my waist and he lifted me until my feet were off the floor. I put my hands on his shoulders and smiled as he spun me around like a child.

"Put me down, you idiot." He kissed me again and sat me down on the table. "Unless you're ready to take the consequences, lady, you better go on up to bed. We can talk more tomorrow."

As he went into the living room to turn out the lamp, I pointed to the picture of the man sitting near the fire. "Mike, will you tell me about that picture tomorrow?"

Mike looked at it for several minutes. "That cabin belonged to my mother's brother, my Uncle John Erhlmann. He was the town doctor. Sally Stonebreaker knew him. She told me that he died the night your great-aunt Madeleine was born. I'll do better than tell you about him. Tomorrow I'll take you to the cabin." He put his arm around me and led me up the stairs to the bedroom.

Before I slipped under the covers, moving quietly so as not to disturb Sally, whose soft breathing I could hear from the next bed, I did something I hadn't done for a very long time. I knelt beside my bed, made the sign of the cross and put my head in my hands. "Help me, Lord, please help me." Not much of a prayer but it had been a long time.

As I settled into bed, turning on my side, I wondered what I should do now. Mike told me that Edward Gerard owned acreage all over Indiana and had partnerships in businesses in three states. He left a considerable inheritance. Because Aunt Jessie had retreated to some safe place in her mind, Mike and I would have to help her. As for the answers to all my questions, it seemed that I would never have them. Sissy had been there when the Munro House burned, but all that Sissy might have told me died with her. As I fell asleep I dreamed I saw her face again. We were eating cheese sandwiches and drinking tea. And she was smiling.

Mike, Sally, and I drove to the cabin an hour after sunup as none of us could sleep past dawn. Mike greeted me with a slow kiss that set my rattled nervous system on edge. We drove down a back road that smelled as if autumn had been distilled into potpourri scattered onto cool air. Mike saw my relaxed look and smiled.

"When my great-grandfather married the Miami woman, White Sky, he built a cabin for her where they could live somewhere between her people and his. Her father was a healer and Indians sometimes came to her because she was known to have his gift. The white people never came. The story is that when she was very young, three or four years of age, a small boy was badly burned. When she heard his cries, she covered his burned leg with her hands and when she removed them, his leg showed no sign of the burn. That was the beginning of her legend in the tribe as a shaman.

She had met Josiah Erhlmann when he traded with her people. He married her by their laws and in his church, and when her people left this area White Sky remained. The white women were afraid to go to her for help and largely shunned her. She had a child and then she died. My great-grandfather lived in that cabin until his death."

"What did White Sky look like?"

Sally answered. "Alice told me they said she was tall for an Indian, with large eyes and beautiful skin. Her hands were small and when healing passed through her, they grew very warm. She was born during a winter when there was heavy snow, and that was how she got her name."

Mike parked the car on a gravel drive that ended near the cabin. Sally and I followed him up the stairs and when he pushed the door open he stepped back and we walked past him into the first of its two rooms. There was an old daguerreotype on the mantle. I walked to the fireplace and touched the image gently.

"That was Tessa, your great-grandmother," Sally said. The woman in the photograph smiled with her eyes as well as her lips. I felt as though she had put out her hand and touched my face just as Sissy had done. My heart ached.

"Alice told me that her son came to get her immediately after he discovered John Erhlmann dead in the stream. She went to the cabin and removed that photo from the mantle because there were those who would have enjoyed a scandal involving

John and his best friend's wife. John left the cabin for Alice to use in her lifetime and then to his sister and his nephew." She smiled at Mike. "Shortly before she died, Alice asked me to replace the photo."

"Were he and my great-grandmother lovers?"

Sally smiled. "No. Your great-grandmother was completely in love with her husband. As for John, well, I'm sure he was in love with her. Worse luck."

Sally went to the stove to fix coffee and Mike and I walked into the small, plain bedroom. A faded quilt covered the iron bed and a crucifix lay on a carved bedside table.

"It's Carl's work," I said, running my fingers over the carving of flowers that formed a border around the top of the table.

"You're right. He gave it to Sally as a birthday gift one year and she asked if she could leave it here."

My fingers were reluctant to leave the carvings. "It reminds me of the desk in your office and some of the furniture in Jessie's house." Tears rushed to my eyes at the thought of something else I had to mourn. I brushed them aside before Mike noticed. We walked out to the porch and looked toward a clearing near the creek where firewood was laid out ready for kindling. We went down the steps toward the fire pit. Sally carried out the coffee in blue metal mugs while Mike lit the fire. We settled on the ground around the fire, sipping coffee. For a brief moment we were far away from the realities that crowded us on every side.

"Oh, God," Mike was staring into the fire which had spurted, throwing fiery crystals into the air above it. He drew his hand across his eyes, removed it, and then stared at the fire again. I put my hand on his arm.

When he looked at me his eyes held a distance I couldn't cross. "What did you see?" My words were a faint whisper.

"This is crazy, Kate. I saw you talking to Kyle. He was setting fire to a teddy bear and you were trying to stop him. Then

I saw you walking through a burning house. There was a fiery pit opening at your feet and across that awful hole was a girl with long, pale hair. She was calling you." Mike shook his head as though to rid himself of his thoughts.

"Look again, Mike." I was beginning to believe many things were possible.

"Nothing there," he cleared his throat. "There never was anything there," he laughed nervously. He glanced at Sally who watched him in silence. Standing up, he threw the dregs of his coffee into the fire. "This has been a long day and I'm beginning to hallucinate from being over-tired."

"It's true, Mike. Kyle did make me burn the toy. I kept telling him I couldn't but he made me do it." Could I have set the house fire, too? I wondered.

Suddenly I remembered the rest of what he saw. "What did she look like, this girl who was calling me?" My need to know made my voice tremble.

"She looked like you, Kate. Her hair was blonde and her eyes were clear and strange, but she looked like you."

Before we left, Mike gave me Tessa's picture. "She belongs to you, Kate. She never was my grandmother and thank the Lord for that! It wouldn't do for us to be cousins." Mike's smile broke the tension that had been building. Sally left the cabin to go to the car. We were alone for a moment and Mike kissed me, a tentative, questioning kiss. I returned it softly. But I felt myself pulling back.

"I've lost so much in the fire, Mike." I fought my tears. "I really am grateful for the picture and for you." His arms held me tightly and his embrace made me feel safe and hopeful. I couldn't know how short a time I would know that peace.

When we returned to Mike's house, there was an envelope in the mailbox. Kendra Caine had invited me to supper. Unless I couldn't come, Carl would pick me up at six o'clock.

Hawks Crossing
1930

The apple tree made scraping sounds against the screen in the bedroom window. They were like worried mutterings of an old friend. Four years earlier David had pulled her away from that window to the warmth of the big white bed with its down comforter and pillows. That tree had been the silent witness to their lovemaking. She remembered the first touch of his hands through her thin, lawn nightdress. There had been a hunger in them when the two made love again and again that first night after their wedding. Lying on her side next to him on the bed, watching him sleep, she had reveled in her happiness, in her nakedness, and in the body he had told her was as soft as silk and filled with excitement and surprises.

This white clapboard house surrounded by its fields was the only home she had ever wanted. She felt its protective embrace as she listened for the sound of his car. Her belly hardened in another useless contraction. Tessa bit her lower lip until it bled, but this time she couldn't deny the pain and her cry echoed through the room and down the stairs. She reached beneath her pillow for her mother's rosary and slipped the beads through her fingers in a wordless prayer.

The sheets were soaked from the breaking of her waters. How long ago? She had lost track of time. Tessa had daydreamed she'd deliver the child before David returned with John Erhlmann. She had imagined how she would smile at David and watch the relief wash over his face when he ran up the stairs and burst into the bedroom. The baby would be safe in the curve of her arm. Now she knew that wasn't possible. If no one helped her, she would die and so would the child inside her. "Mother of God, pray for us sinners now and at the hour of our death," she cried aloud. The pain stopped for a moment and she sucked in a satisfying breath of the cool air stirring the curtains. The breeze carried with it a barely discernible jangle of cowbells.

Tessa's mind grasped at the sound as though it were a hand she could cling to in her struggle. She had painted flowered bells for their small herd to remind her of Kitzbuhl, where she was born. In the mountains of Austria, in a world of clear blue skies and endless spaces, she had been the center of her mama and papa's universe. Then her papa died. Mama buried him with the rest of his family who rested one above another in a single grave. Her world changed.

She remembered the small iron fences around the graves near the church and the vigil lights, fixed to poles, flickering above them. When she had knelt at Papa's grave, weeping and lost, Mama had lifted her up and with tears sliding down her cheeks, told Tessa that Papa loved her and now that he was in paradise, he would watch over both of them even more tenderly.

Once she dreamed of showing her own children the paths where Papa had carried her on his shoulders. But that might never happen. What if she died bearing this child? The small cemetery beside St. Mary Church in Hawks Crossing, a little distance from the edge of their woods, would be her burial place. At least she would lie near Mama's grave.

Her mama. Tessa thought of the full arms and soft blue eyes that were her constant refuge when they left Kitzbuhl after

Papa's death. They had traveled far to Uncle Froney's home in America, to Indiana, and when he died, they stayed in the small house he left to them. She fingered the mother of pearl beads her mother had counted her prayers on every evening of their lives. Even now, the memory of Eva, her mama, comforted her. She remembered her in the garden, large and blonde with arms full of the tall, speckled flowers for their table.

Tessa loved those flowers. They were part of long nights of making love in this room. David said that her skin reminded him of lilies. Not the white lilies of Easter, but the, freckled tiger lilies of summer. She had discarded her thin cotton nightgown almost at once. David loved to feel her smooth body next to his night after night. He must plant tiger lilies on my grave, she thought, lots of tiger lilies. David's face filled her mind until she could almost touch him. Who would help David?

At once, as though in answer to her question, John Erhlmann's eyes were looking into hers. His eyes were strange, the dilated pupils surrounded by thin, golden brown irises. It was comforting to look up and see them resting on her, and they did so often. But then he had always been her rock.

One October evening when Emily's little body had been hot with fever and David was in Indianapolis, John had stayed with the child. He had a strange gift, one that allowed him to treat illness with his touch as much as with his medicines. Tessa remembered how Emily's restlessness had stopped after John stroked her face and arms and laid his hand on her head. Because she was still feverish, he stayed the night, stretching out on the sofa until the child's pillow was soaked in the morning and her body, blessedly cool.

He had also been with Tessa through a frightening time when David fought the influenza that took his mother.

Old Dr. Erhlmann, who had helped her with Emily's delivery, was dead now, so she asked John to help her if she could not deliver the child herself. Her mama had been a midwife in Austria and Tessa had helped her deliver babies here in Hawks

Crossing. She was so proud of her mama's soothing presence and the calm with which she delivered the babies. Tessa was confident she could deliver this child.

John's eyes had held hers when she told him that. It pleased her that he did not doubt her ability to handle a normal delivery. His concern was for the unexpected. Remembering his face as he listened to her, Tessa wondered if John Erhlmann was in love with her. It was a troubling thought, yet it might be true. She realized, not for the first time, that she might have fallen in love with John Erhlmann but for David. John was a man with deep feelings, a person of great intellect, even mystery, but he wasn't David. For her it must always be David.

Thoughts of John Erhlmann flowed out of her consciousness as she yearned for her little daughter. Tessa's heart ached for the pain she would cause soft-eyed, softhearted Emily. The child imitated her every move, her every word. Emily brushed her mama's hair and brought her dolls to tea parties that she and Tessa planned. And every night she asked Tessa to sing to her after she was tucked into bed. "Sing a song of sixpence, a pocket full of rye. . . ." Who will sing to her when I'm gone, Tessa wondered and tears spilled from her eyes. The child was too young to be comforted. She knew how much Emily would suffer. She remembered herself at that age, frightened and confused, standing at her father's grave.

Emily and the baby would miss her, but David would suffer the most. Her throat tightened and tears slipped down her cheeks as she thought of him. But inside her, there was no trace of despair. She was certain God would bring them together again. God had made them from the same thought and neither could ever be complete again alone. Because of David, she already knew something of paradise.

She rested her hand on her stomach and prayed for her baby. Her body was quiet and she let her mind drift. She was standing with this little girl on the porch, watching the morning sky turning pink and pearl above the barn. She was playing with her under the red plum tree when a roll of thunder turned their heads toward the storm gathering over the fields. She was walking with her in the little herb garden near the back door, crushing fragrant leaves in her hand and holding them to the girl's face. Tessa closed her eyes and saw herself guide a small hand to touch Lolly's velvet nose before she pulled the child up in front of her and rode the mare across their fields. She watched her eating the blackberries that grew in brambles along the wood line. She played hide and seek under the arbor heavy with grapes. Tessa never doubted the child inside her was another beautiful daughter. "Maddy," she whispered to her. "Maddy, I love you."

Pain knifed between her legs. Something was wrong. Emily's birth had been so easy, not like this. Her back arched and her body burned. "David," she whispered, "David."

With the ease of a butterfly catching a soft breeze, she fell into a deep place, a pond of coolness where she floated without effort and without pain. She heard someone calling and she reached up toward the light. A child was there, a beautiful child with strange, pale eyes and an expression of peace. The child took her hand and spoke to her.

Tessa looked up in wonder. The child smiled and touched her face. Together they walked downstairs toward the kitchen where grapes were boiling for jelly. She wanted to tell Emily something. She had to be sure Emily knew the liquid must reach a rolling boil before it could be poured into the clean Ball jars. The scent filled the air around her, making her smile. She breathed deeply and thought she heard the sound of bells.

"I saved the baby, David but I couldn't save Tessa." Above his beard John's face was gray with fatigue. He couldn't stop the bleeding. He had tried until there was nothing more to do. The blood kept seeping out, darkening the gauze packing, her life running in small rivulets down his hands. He had washed his hands repeatedly in the white bowl on the bedroom bureau. They were still damp. "Emily has a tiny sister."

The man sitting on the landing of the stairs outside the bedroom never raised his head. "What will I do now?" he asked in a strangled voice. "Tessa was my life. There isn't anything else."

"Yes, there is." Erhlmann heard his own words as though from a distance. "There's Emily and this new little girl. You must build a life for them now." He sat next to David. "And there's something else." David's bloodshot gaze moved slowly from his friend's damp hands to his face. "There's something wrong with the child's legs." A tear slid down David's cheek. "My God," he said. "Tessa died to bear a crippled child."

His head snapped back from the slap administered by Erhlmann's hand. "She would do it again. You know how much she wanted this child. Life doesn't always give us our desires; it just gives or takes away." His cheek bearing the red welt of the blow, David looked into bloodshot, anguish-filled eyes and saw the truth staring back at him. Tessa was gone but the little child she left behind was a piece of her. Rubbing one hand across his eyes, he tried to rise above the wave of hopelessness that was drowning him. "Tessa, Tessa," he kept crying in his head. "My life is over, there is nothing more to look forward to, nothing more to want." Erhlmann's eyes held him like a vice, keeping him from falling, from running away. "Leave me alone with her."

Tessa was lying in the middle of their bed, not in her usual place closer to the window. The long hair he loved lay limply on one of the pillowcases. Her eyes were closed and seemed to have dark shadows around them, but her mouth was still the sweet curve he would always desire, its lower lip full and round with a small bruised corner. The touch of her lips was cool and familiar.

He whispered to her and laid his head on her still breast. She had asked him if they could name the baby Madeleine if she had a girl. She had intended to call her Maddy. Poor little Maddy. He lifted his head to look at the tiny girl in the bassinet. Her body was wrapped in a flannel blanket and her arms and neck were still covered with bits of a thin, cheesy-like substance that John had not had the time to clean completely. One arm moved in a jerky motion, the other was relaxed. Her legs did not move at all. Two blue eyes stared up at him unblinkingly. A rush of memory engulfed him; Tessa, lying next to him, cupping his hand around the small bulge in her swollen stomach. He had held her carefully, bracing himself so as not to put his weight on her, his hands exploring the incredible softness of her skin, making love gently so as not to hurt the little one in any way.

For a moment, he closed his eyes in a sudden spasm of pain. Had his lovemaking caused the baby to be born with useless legs? Had he caused it all? Everything? Even Tessa's death? His mind careened in despair, trying to find something to keep the sensation of drowning away. "God help me," he prayed fiercely. "Why did you take her and leave me? I'm lost without her. What am I to do now? Oh, God!"

John Erhlmann winced at the sound of David's hoarse weeping. He opened a cabinet in Tessa's yellow and blue kitchen and took out a can of coffee. He kept his thoughts carefully in the little room in his mind where he had learned to hide his love for Tessa. He had years of practice. Only a little longer now and he could leave the house and be alone with the emptiness gnawing inside him.

A pitcher filled with lilacs stood in the middle of the table. They were very fresh. She must have picked them that morning. He brushed them lightly; wondering if his fingers rested where hers had touched. A baby's bottle stood beside the pitcher. "I'm going to nurse my baby, John," she had said, "but help me with a formula just in case." He ached for the sound of that voice, the way she smiled with her eyes before she spoke. He put the percolator on the stove and then he heated some water to sterilize the bottle.

It was Madeleine's crying, a soft whimpering, that woke David. He had fallen asleep next to Tessa, his arm across her motionless body. "I love you, Tessa," he said softly into one small ear. He pulled his arm away from her unyielding body, smiled down at her face, then softly laid the white sheet over it. He wrapped the tiny crying child more tightly in the receiving blanket Tessa had hemmed for her and took her downstairs.

John was standing at the stove heating a small bottle of milk. David looked at him in a weak, dazed way, holding the mewing baby in his arms. "I'm going to need some help. Maybe tomorrow I'll be able to figure it out. Who can take Tessa's place with the children?" His voice broke and the cold emptiness spread inside his chest. He felt like a piece of stone. "No one will ever take her place. No one, David. But you will need help. Let me think about it awhile." John's eyes narrowed as he considered the problem.

David had never felt so alone. "Help me tell Emily," he said to the memory of Tessa's face in his mind. "Help me make her understand that you didn't want to leave, that we'll see you again. Help me hide my bitterness, my anger against God, against you for leaving me. Help me love them enough. Whatever Maddy's problems are, make me strong enough to help her, to be there for her, and to keep her from pain and sadness."

John watched the dark head droop as David moved farther inward and farther away from him in his grief. David's pain, he knew was worse than his. He had never held Tessa close to him, never made love to her and felt her eager response. He had never lain next to her through winter nights, warming himself with her body, never wakened to her next to him when the spring rain beat on the roof. Only David knew what it was like to miss her with his whole body as well as his heart. John Erhlmann, who knew nothing of such joys, only knew he had to face life completely alone and without hope of seeing her again. He had to live without his secret, guilty thoughts that if something should happen to David, he would be there to take care of Tessa. He had always known that but for David, Tessa would have loved him. About the children, he could not think at all. They were all that was left of her and they belonged, as she had, to David. In time they might share their mother's ability to stir love, her capacity for loving life. They might be like her but that would not bring him peace. Nothing could bring him peace after he had been unable to stop the bleeding.

He had been in love with Tessa Zahler ever since they had sat next to each other in the frame high school east of town. She had studied algebra with him, tried to teach him to polka, cheered when he gave the valedictorian address, laughed at his unexpected kiss one New Year's Eve and never saw the way his eyes gave him away when he looked at her. For her there was always and only David McLaren. He knew he should have married, but he couldn't offer another girl the heart and soul he gave to Tessa when he was eighteen.

John took the baby from David's arms and placed her in a corner of the sofa. He put a cup of coffee in his friend's hands and went upstairs to get the bassinet.

John closed the door of the bedroom and knelt beside the bed. He pulled the sheet from Tessa's face and shoulders and willed the image of her to burn into his mind. There was no need for a final gesture. The moment after she died, he had leaned down to press his mouth against hers. He looked at the stillness of her, the oval of her face, her unforgettable skin. "Good-bye, Tessa," he said, and covered her face. When he could breathe again, he took the bassinet, a clean sheet and blanket, and went downstairs.

When John left the house, David was sitting in Tessa's rocking chair, feeding the baby and making a groaning, crooning noise as he moved back and forth.

That night Emily came home from a neighbor's house where she had gone to play. It broke David's heart to watch her say goodbye to Tessa. She smoothed her mommy's hair and put her round cheek to Tessa's still lips. "Mommy won't like it in heaven, Daddy, cause she'll miss us. She'll come back. Don't cry, baby," Emily said to her sleeping sister, though her own round cheeks were shiny with the tears that gushed when she sobbed. "Mommy is an angel now so I will be Mommy for both of us until she comes home. Daddy says we must be careful not to hurt you cause your legs don't work." She leaned closer to one tiny ear. "I'll be your legs, baby. I'll be your legs and take you everyplace."

On his way home, John Erhlmann made a single stop. There were lights in the windows of the Munro House and Alice Munro came to the door.

Later, after he left her, he drove to his small brick house just outside of town and took a bottle of bourbon from the pantry. He had been blind drunk only twice in his life: once when David married Tessa and once when Emily was born. But those nights had not held the despair he faced this night. The pain in his belly gnawed at him and his chest was heavy with tears he couldn't cry—tears that crushed him like stone. He drove the narrow gravel and dirt roads to the cabin his grandfather had built beside one of the little streams formed where Lost River left its underground bed and rose to the surface. He hit the brakes quickly and barely missed a deer that leaped across the road, flashing through his headlights. He wished it had struck him. The old car couldn't have taken the blow and all of his pain would have ended.

He passed a stand of pine trees on his left just beyond a small cave where his mother used to keep her preserves. One summer, gypsies had camped in fields near the cabin and had stolen her precious jars. He wished now that the gypsies had stolen him. All of the children had been threatened with that possibility to keep them away from strangers. If he had left this place when he was ten, he would never have met Tessa and she would still be alive.

John stood in front of the fireplace and raised his glass to the picture in the carved mahogany frame on the mantle above it. It began to rain as he poured more whiskey into his glass. As long as he could see Tessa now and then, listen to her talk and help her with the children, he could pretend she belonged to him and he had a reason to live. "Oh God, what am I supposed to do now?" The words were wrenched from him like rusted nails ripped from boards where they had been deeply imbedded.

Eventually the liquor began to burn and blunt the edge of pain knifing his insides. The next few drinks were better because his head was beginning to feel light. He walked out on the porch, down the steps, and into the rain that fell in tiny blows on his hair and shoulders. He sat on a large stone near the edge of the water and waited. He felt his buttocks and legs dissolve into the wetness of the rock under him and the rain, heavier now, pounded and plastered his shirt to his back and chest. He shivered. For a moment, he was absorbed into the rain and the cool night air and there was no space in his brain for her, not even in that little room with its tightly closed door. It would be easy to stay here, like this, with no thoughts and no feelings, just becoming one with the endless rain, like the rocks underneath him.

When he was a boy, his father told him stories of Miami Indians who camped near here. One of them, a female ancestor of his reputed to be a healer, was able to read the past and the future in the smoke of sacred fires. What he would give this moment to have that power! As a boy he had loved the memory of his grandmother, White Sky, and was filled with a peculiar certainty that she had seen him in her fires and for his sake left a sense of herself in the cabin and in him. He felt that when he was ill or troubled or bringing relief to the sick.

White Sky had become a Christian when she married Josiah Erhlmann and the small crucifix he gave her on her baptismal day lay on the table beside the bed. Sometimes it was the only bed where John could find dreamless, restful sleep. Sometimes he held the crucifix and thought he felt warmth as from the touch of a hand. So often he had wanted to share the peace and beauty of this place with Tessa. He had turned on the phonograph before he left the cabin and he could hear Mozart's 12th piano concerto through the rain. He closed his eyes.

Suddenly he heard her calling him. "Tessa? Where are you? "He looked back to the cabin and saw her standing on the porch by the open door, motioning him to come in, the smile starting in her eyes. He stood up and stared at the vision as it disappeared. He smiled back at her. That was part of it, of course. He hallucinated when he got drunk. He was hoping just for this, for another moment with her. John Erhlmann raised his glass to the woman standing on the empty porch. He shook his head to clear the rain from his eyes and the motion caused him to lose his balance. He felt himself slipping and saw her running to him, her arms outstretched. He smiled and reached for her as the glass shattered, a sound lost in the music and the blowing rain. A red stain flowed from his temple as, unconscious, he slipped into the water and drowned.

About six o'clock the next morning David heard a knock at the door. He was preparing formula and before he could answer it, Alice Munro stepped into the room, her smooth brown hair brushed back from a thin face whose skin was remarkably unlined. Tessa had always said it was the result of having her hair pulled back—it gave her friend a sort of face-lift. David had laughed when Tessa promised him that when she grew older, she would wear her hair that way. Now she would never grow older.

Kendra, her face serious as always, followed her grandmother into the room. She was a plain child of Emily's age. Alice pulled a sweater from around her shoulders, hung it on the back of a kitchen chair and stood for a moment watching David. Her eyes were soft with affection and sadness. "I'm so sorry about Tessa, so sorry. Doc told me some hours ago but he said I was not to bother you until morning." David stopped stirring the milk a moment and his eyes filled with tears, but he did not answer her. Feeling her small hand on his shoulder, he turned and looked down into her face, at her wet cheeks. Her arms went around him and they both cried.

In her early fifties, with a grown son and a three-year-old granddaughter, Alice still had the eyes and the slim bearing of a much younger woman. She had lost two little boys to influenza during a particularly raw Indiana winter. Another child, a little girl, had been unable to survive beyond a year. Only her son Kenneth had lived to manhood. Now principal of Hawks Crossing High School, he was married to his high school sweetheart, Diane, and was Kendra's father. Unfortunately Diane was a selfish mother, reluctant to share the child with her mother-in-law.

After Claude Munro died, Alice remained alone at the Munro House and hired Sally Stonebreaker to help with housework twice a week. The sturdy eighteen-year old with a wide smile that showed pretty teeth and a good deal of the pink gum above them, brought hope with her when she came in the back door on Tuesdays and Thursdays. Alice knew what that sunny face could mean to two little girls who faced life without their mother.

"Kendra, please go to Emily's room and wake her for breakfast." Obedient as always, the child bent her head and went to do her grandmother's bidding.

Alice poured two cups of coffee and put them on the table where a yellow pitcher held three sprays of drooping lilacs. Tears burned her eyes as she realized that one of the last things Tessa did before going upstairs was to cut these flowers to make her kitchen beautiful. They were dead now, like Tessa, she thought, their beauty faded, and their fragrance gone. She went to the back porch, opened the door and emptied the vase of its water. Reluctantly, she threw the flowers into the trash sack just inside the door.

A few moments later, she turned on the stove, put butter in a skillet, broke eggs into a bowl, scrambled them with milk, salt, and pepper, and added them to the melting butter. David filled a baby's bottle with heated milk, screwed on the nipple and put it in Alice's outstretched hand. She sprinkled some of the milk on her wrist. "Let it stand a few minutes and it will be fine. Now, please, sit down, David, I want to talk to you and you need some breakfast."

He sat down heavily and picked up his cup, his expression fixed and distant. Alice's voice brought him back from the memory where he was hiding.

"Have you given any thought to what you must do now that . . . now that Tessa's gone? Who will care for the baby and Emily?"

David shook his head. "There's no family left to help me, Alice. I'll have to hire a woman to take care of the children and to keep house for me." At the thought of it, his forehead grew wrinkled and deep lines formed between his sunken, red eyes.

She continued to move the eggs with a spatula and called to the girls to come to the table. "David, I want you to listen to me. I think the best thing for you to do would be to let me help you with the children." He looked up at her with surprise.

"You don't want the work of raising children again, Alice. You don't need the income. You have a settled life." She brushed his words aside with a wave of her hand.

"Of course, I don't need the money. But what's so wonderful about my 'settled life,' David? What I need is something to do with my life, something to make my days full and happy again. You know how much I love children. There's Kendra, of course, but I spend so little time with her." She looked away.

She put the eggs on three plates, poured two glasses of milk and cut slices of a loaf of bread on which she smoothed a layer of jelly. Kendra and Emily came downstairs. Emily kissed her father and the baby and gave Alice a hug. Sleepy-eyed, her hair tousled, she was not quite fully awake. Just looking at her made Alice's heart ache.

While the children ate, Alice and David sat in the front room. She looked at him earnestly.

"I'm lonely, David, and I'm looking for meaning in my

life. You're alone now and looking for help with the children. Please, at least say you'll think about it. I'll have Sally spend one day a week doing your housework and Emily and the baby will spend some of their time here and some at my house. You know how Tessa loved my house. And you know how much I loved her. You and Tessa and Emily are like my own family. The baby will be just one more piece of Tessa to love. What have you named the child?"

"Madeleine," he said. "Tessa named her for a character in a book." His words broke on a stifled sob. She bent her head to hide her own tears. Alice felt David's arms around her and they cried together.

"They can call me Auntie Alice," she said.

It was a full day later before Kenneth Munro found John Erhlmann's body. At his mother's insistence, Kenneth disposed of the bottle of bourbon and the shattered glass beside the body before he reported the death to the sheriff. The official report showed that John was caught in the rain walking back to his cabin when he slipped and fell to his death. Except for the cabin, John's will left his small estate to Indiana University Medical School.

The night after he found John, Kenneth sat talking with Diane in their small kitchen. Kendra, aware of the strange excitement in her parents' voices, tiptoed out of her room and stood in the dark hallway listening.

"You should have told the authorities, Kenny. He was drunk and that was that."

"What would be the point? Why ruin his good name? Delivering the baby and watching Tessa die was just too much for him. It would be for anybody."

"You know it was more than that, Kenny. John Erhlmann was in love with David's wife."

Kenneth noticed she never could bear to say Tessa's

name, even now when she was dead. He knew of his wife's jealousy of Tessa, but was never quite sure if it was her happiness she envied or something else. His mind never went to that place. He decided long ago to lay it up to Diane's inability to enjoy life. "People should pay for what they do," she was saying.

"Stop it, Di. Give your imaginings a rest. She's dead now." He looked into his wife's agitated face. Her cheeks were pale and her eyes red-rimmed. Her expression made her thin, angular face unpleasant to look at. He knew she wasn't crying for Tessa.

"Kenny, she wasn't beyond looking for affection outside her own house. Why, I wouldn't be surprised if the baby was John's after all."

Kendra started at the anger in her father's voice. "Stop it, Diane! I knew John Erhlmann. He would never touch another man's wife. And there wasn't a chance Tessa would love anyone but David. If I ever hear you say such a thing again I swear I'll have elder Curtis here to remind you of your duty as a Christian woman."

Barefooted, Kendra tiptoed silently back to her bedroom. She shut the door and slipped into bed, pulling the sheets over her head to stop the sound of her mother's crying. She hated to hear her cry. Her mother was often unhappy, and the weeping was worse tonight. Kendra felt her own tears slip down her cheeks and make damp places on her pillow. She hated the dead woman who made her mother so sad.

Alice Munro got permission from John's sister to purchase a special headstone carved with his name, date of death, the words, "beloved friend and physician" and two hawks in flight. As she looked at the stone she remembered the evening she found John drunk in the woods near St. Mary's church. It was Tessa and David's wedding day. Alice sat on the ground beside him and listened to his disjointed story of hopeless love.

He never gave any indication that he remembered that night or how she had cried with him and then helped him to his cabin where he woke up the next day.

Alice sighed. The day Claude Munro married her she stood beside him in her white linen dress, holding a bouquet of lilies of the valley, and knowing, even as he put the ring on her finger, that he didn't get the girl he wanted. That girl, Francey Maron, married someone else.

Every Sunday of their married life when they walked to services, Claude tipped his hat to Francey who bent her head in acknowledgement. Then Francey would look at her and touch her raw wound with that look. Every Sunday she knew what it meant to be a man's second choice. She looked in the mirror at hair that wasn't as long or as curling as Francey's black hair. But the most bitter thing of all was watching that woman bring all her children to sit beside her at the service. Alice knew that Claude somehow believed that she should have been able to prevent the illnesses that took their George and Jeffery. Her heart ached remembering George's two-year-old sturdy little body. Sometimes she still dreamed of the two little boys she had lost to the epidemic. She didn't need the photo on her bureau to remember them. She would feel Jeff's mouth against her breast and for a few blessed moments she knew the joy of being all in all to another living creature. Through all the years after the tragedy, she tried to make Claude love her. Then he was gone and it was too late. Slowly she learned how to live without the sight of his face and without the daily fear of being a failure. She began to trust herself to build her life again and to know some measure of contentment. Tessa, Emily, and John had provided much of that happiness.

Her friends thought Alice had the mason carve hawks on the stone to symbolize the town, but to her they were John and Tessa paired perpetually in stone, though never in life. Sometimes she even thought they represented herself and Claude as they might have been had she been able to make him love her. It was always about love, Alice thought, and about one's failures at it.

After the funeral Mass David and Emily led the procession of mourners to the small graveyard. The people followed the coffin in two lines. "Hail Mary, full of grace, the Lord is with thee, blessed art thou among women and blessed is the fruit of thy womb, Jesus." Those on the left answered, "Holy Mary, mother of God, pray for us sinners now and at the hour of our death. Amen."

Diane made a face as the prayers droned on and glanced down at Kendra who was listening intently. She whispered into her husband's ear but he just looked at her, his mouth tightening, and said nothing. After the final prayers were said and the casket lowered into the earth, David turned from the grave, unable to throw his handful of earth against it. Emily looked at the funeral bouquets that were being tossed into the grave and pulled on her daddy's sleeve. "Mommy doesn't want those flowers, Daddy. She wants tiger lilies, lots of tiger lilies." David stooped to pick up his daughter and looked into her wide eyes. "How do you know that, Em," he asked softly. "Mommy told me last night, Daddy. When I was sleeping she sat on my bed and sang the sixpence song and told me that when I came to talk to her in the churchyard I should bring her tiger lilies. Can we plant some by her stone?"

He looked at her serious little face and understood why she had not cried in church or at the grave. A heaviness lifted from his chest. "Did she say anything else, Em?

"Oh, yes, Daddy. She said she would be close to me and that if I paid attention, I might still be able to see her once in awhile." Emily hugged her father. "Don't cry, Daddy, Mommy's fine and she said sometime we'll all be together. You and me and Maddy and Mommy."

From a distance, Alice watched the two heads so close together, comforting each other. She walked with Kenneth, Diane, and Kendra as they turned to follow the second coffin.

As they stood at John's grave, she heard Diane's sharp whisper. "When did John become a Catholic? Was that just another sign of his 'friendship' for Tessa, too?" Kenneth turned away from her and Alice was stunned by the naked grief on her daughter-in-law's face. She wondered in what fantasy her daughter-in-law was indulging. She was certain John had never given her a reason for such grief.

In Diane Munro's memory, John Erhlmann was standing on her porch on a cool spring night. He had examined Kendra and diagnosed nothing more than a case of measles. As he assured Diane that the child was in no real danger, he saw the lines in her tired face and put his arm around her shoulders in a quick hug. In a moment, her arms had wound around his neck and had pulled his face to hers. Her kiss was not returned, and when he pushed her away, gently but firmly, his face had hardened.

"Let's pretend that never happened, Diane. You're just tired and overwrought. Good-bye, now, I'm due at Tessa and David's for supper. You can call me there if you need me."

Diane shut her eyes at the memory. When she opened them, she saw her mother-in- law's curious expression. As she moved from the grave, Diane took Kendra's hand and led her away from her grandmother. The girl looked at her mother's angry face and back at the churchyard. "You don't like this church. You don't like David or Emily either, do you, Momma? Why not?"

"They're not like us, Kendra. They have strange ways and they are not nice people."

Kendra's little face worked in a frown. "Then I shouldn't like them, either, Momma, should I?"

"No, Kendra, you shouldn't like them either." Bending down, she pulled Kendra to her in a rare embrace and the girl's heart felt as though it would burst with happiness. All she ever wanted was to have her momma love her. Maybe it was not so hard. From that moment, she disliked David, Emily, Maddy, and all the strange people who went to pray in St. Mary's Church.

The summer Maddy turned four, Emily sat on the porch next to her sister's padded chair. Maddy's long blonde hair fell straight and shiny to her shoulders. Her face was intent on her drawing; she held the pad against her right arm and drew with her stronger left hand. "What are you drawing?" Emily asked, her short, curly head of red hair leaning close with seven-year-old curiosity.

"Drawing the nest in that tree, Em." She put down the crayon and sighed. "I wish I could climb it. See how that branch moves a little in the wind—like a swing?" Em thought a minute as her eyes followed her sister's finger. She wondered if she could do it. She might fall. That would make Auntie Alice mad, and Daddy's eyes would have that sad look that made her feel like crying. But she had made a promise to Mommy that she had to keep, a promise always to take care of Maddy.

"Would you like me to get that nest down? Could you draw it better if it was closer?" Em pointed to a brown robin's nest near the top of the tree. She thought the branch might be just big enough to hold her.

"Oh, yes," Maddy's wide eyes were fixed on the nest. Pulling a porch chair close to the sugar maple, Em pulled herself into the crotch of the tree, and then slowly reached up for the next branch. The bark cut her hands, but she bit her tongue and kept climbing. She knew she shouldn't look down, but she heard Maddy laughing and she did. Looking down made her dizzy, but she held tight with both arms.

"It's fun, Maddy," she called, taking a deep breath. The branches were becoming smaller but she still kept climbing. Her overalls were keeping her knees from hurting like her hands. When she was close to the nest, she almost fell trying to reach it. Stifling a cry, she held on tight and her eyes suddenly caught sight of a face at her daddy's bedroom window. The face was framed in long dark hair and smiled encouragingly. One hand was pressed against the glass as if to touch her. She closed her eyes tightly and looked again. She caught the reflection of her own face. Reaching out again, she grabbed the small cluster of twigs and leaves. "Got it, Maddy, got it," she yelled. Coming down was harder, but she knew she could make it. She glanced up at the window and smiled. "Thanks for helping me, Mommy." When she felt the chair under her feet, she stopped to look up at the tall tree she had climbed. "We have a secret, she said. You saw Mommy, too, didn't you?" She put her arms around the gnarled trunk in a hug. Then she ran to give Maddy the robin's nest.

That night at the oak table in the kitchen, Maddy gave Em her finished drawing of the bird's nest. "Why, Maddy, that's good," Em said. "Daddy, will you make a frame so I can hang it in our room?"

"Sure, honey," David said. "Maddy you did a good job drawing the nest. Every little piece looks real."

"Em got it for me," Maddy said, looking at her big sister with a smile.

Auntie Alice looked up from the soup she was stirring. "Em, did you climb that old tree? You'll break your neck, child." Em did not meet her daddy's eyes. His worried look hurt her. She wanted him to tell her she was right to climb that tree, to be Maddy's legs. She wanted to tell him about Mommy, but something made her bite her tongue before she did. Sometimes, when he talked about Mommy, his eyes grew strange and fixed and she had the funny feeling he wasn't looking at her anymore.

"You and Maddy are all I have, Emily. You mustn't get hurt. It would make me worry if I thought you did dangerous things. Please don't climb that tree again. I know that it's tempting. It was your mother's favorite tree, especially in autumn."

"I know," Em said softly, remembering the face in the window. She said a quick prayer. "Help me, Mommy. I know it's a sin to disobey Daddy but I can't promise I'll never climb that tree again, I can't." She walked over to where her daddy sat in the rocking chair with a newspaper in his lap. She put her hand on his cheek. "Don't worry, Daddy. I'm fine. Mommy is my special angel taking care of me."

"Me, too," Maddy said in her soft voice.

David lifted Em on his lap and kissed both her cheeks. "You look like her, Em," he whispered so Maddy wouldn't hear and be jealous. "Except for your red hair, you look so much like her."

On Sundays, they always ate lunch at Auntie Alice's house. Everyone in town called it the Munro House. It was the oldest house in the county and Em loved its red brick, its flat Italianate roof and the wide porch that wrapped around it. Maddy's favorite room was the little semi-circular music room where she would cuddle on the satin love seat with its gold fleur de lis pattern and listen to Auntie Alice play the shiny black piano. She called it a baby grand.

It was Kendra who loved her grandmother's house most, though secretly. Every demilune table with curved legs was a joy for her to dust, and the crystal and the dishes in the breakfront made her catch her breath. She noticed how the old crystal chandelier in the parlor sparkled when the sunlight touched it as it came through the beveled glass windows. When no one was looking, she touched the stained glass forest scene in one beautiful window.

There was a jewelry box that played Edelweiss on her grandmother's dressing table and in it were pieces of jewelry made in Germany by one of her grandma's great-uncles. Even with her eyes closed she could see them: an amethyst brooch, two lockets made of rose gold on thin, shining chains, one matching gold bracelet with a locket charm, a garnet ring and a pair of pearl earrings set with diamonds. She could hardly wait to see them.

As part of the Sunday visits, Alice Munro would let the girls handle the jewelry. Em and Maddy always exclaimed over their beauty and begged to try them on. Only Kendra was quiet when she touched them. "I guess they're all right, grandmother, but I really don't like jewelry. I think it's nicer to have a pretty dress for Sunday services." She remembered what her mother had told her every time she helped her into her best dress for the visit.

"Don't fuss over her things, Kendra, or she will think you and I are greedy and can't wait until she's dead so we can have them." Kendra was always shocked when her mother talked that way. She wondered why her mother thought grandmother would think that about the two of them. She loved her grandmother. But every Sunday, Diane reminded her not to seem too interested and just to remember that it would all be theirs anyway when her grandmother died. After awhile, Kendra began to think those thoughts as though they were her own. Alice Munro was always surprised and a little hurt at the girl's inability to appreciate her beautiful things.

Time for our tea, girls," she would say. "Would you like to pour, Kendra?"

Pointing to the flowered porcelain teapot, she smiled at her solemn-faced granddaughter. "No, thank you. I might break it." Coaxing did not change her mind, so Em would pour while Kendra held back tears of disappointment. Still, every Sunday night, when Diane brushed her hair, she could honestly say that she had not shown any interest in her grandmother's things and that would bring a rare smile to Diane's face. The child needed that smile more than the touch of lovely teapots and golden lockets. Her task from God, she was sure, was to make her mother happy.

"It's your ninth birthday, tomorrow, and I have a special present for you," Sally said. She settled Maddy in Alice's old wagon and hitched up the sorrel that pulled it for hayrides and sleigh rides and very special days.

"Since your daddy and Emily are off buying you a present, I'm going to give you my present today. It's a story, Maddy, and a place where you can draw a picture after I tell it."

Maddy's face seemed to radiate light as she anticipated this treat. Wearing a tee shirt and overalls, with her sketchbook on her lap, she looked even younger than her nine years, Sally thought. She felt the strong bond between herself and the child growing every day. Maddy often gave her some of her sketches in return for an hour of storytelling that held the child like a spell. At those moments, Sally felt strong and in her own place, like the tall, golden tiger lilies that bloomed in prideful abandon along one side of the house. She felt protective of Maddy, her heart aching for the girl's weak legs. She often told Alice that Maddy was like a little sister to her.

That afternoon was the first time Maddy saw the cabin where John Erhlmann had died. She knew that the doctor who delivered her was her parents' friend and had died suddenly in an accident on the night of her birth. Because Auntie Alice was his special friend, he had left the cabin and the land around it to her. She knew that, too.

It was cool and pleasant in the shade around the cabin when Sally took Maddy's chair out of the wagon and lifted her down into it. The strength of the older girl and the frailty of the younger made such transfers possible, but Sally felt a twinge of sadness in her chest, knowing that soon she would be unable to handle Maddy by herself. Wheeling her to the porch, she lifted her again into one of two armchairs from the cabin that she had placed there the night before. Between them was a small table on which she laid the contents of the wicker basket that had shared the space in the wagon with Maddy's chair.

"You're wonderful, Sally, I love picnics," the little girl said as Sally set out a plate of sandwiches she had made that morning, along with two bottles of coke, a bag of potato chips, and fresh chocolate chip cookies wrapped in a napkin. Maddy helped herself to half a sandwich of chicken salad smothered in mayonnaise and smiled at Sally. "But I love your stories more."

"The story I'm going to tell you is a special story, Maddy, because it's not made up. It really happened." Sally chewed her sandwich thoughtfully and took a sip of coke. Maddy knew better than to rush her. Sally said stories had to be told at their own pace.

"Well, Maddy, you know that Doc John used to own this cabin. It had been his daddy's cabin and his granddaddy's before him. What most folks don't know is how it came to be built. That's the secret I want to share with you. I learned it from your Auntie Alice and she said I could tell you.

You learned at school that years and years ago, there were Indian tribes living all over this land. While most white people gave them a wide berth, some traded with them and made friends with them. One of those white men was Doc John's grandfather, Josiah Erhlmann, who fell in love with an Indian girl named White Sky. He married her both by Indian law and by the law of his Christian church. He built this cabin for her, and when her people moved away, she chose to stay with him." Sally leaned forward and her voice became so soft that Maddy had to listen carefully to understand what she was saying.

"White Sky was a very special woman. She had the power of healing in her and she was able to read the fires." Maddy's eyes widened and then narrowed as she thought about it.

"What does that mean, Sally?"

"I'm not sure, exactly, but I think it means she could see things in the fire—things that might happen in the future or things that were the answer to questions people asked her."

"Like an oracle," Maddy said in awe. "I've been reading Em's book about the Oracle of Delphi. I didn't know Indians had oracles, too."

"I'm not sure it's the same thing, Maddy," Sally said. Although she had graduated from high school, she had read only what was demanded and forgotten most of that. Her loves were housework and telling stories other people had told her. She spent hours talking to the oldest people in the town and had committed their family histories to memory. About the oracles of Greece, she had no knowledge.

"Do you think she looked in the fire and saw us sitting here on her porch tonight?"

"I don't know." Sally said with a grin. "But if she did, she probably would be glad to see us having such a good time." Maddy laughed.

"Now," Sally said, "Here's my surprise. I'm going to light that wood by the water's edge, so you can see what it would have looked like when White Sky read her fires. I'll sit next to it with my back to you and you can pretend I'm her and draw a wonderful picture for me. Will you?"

Maddy wiped the last trace of chocolate from her lips with her napkin and stretched out her stronger arm as if embracing the entire afternoon. Then she smiled and shook her head.

The wood was very dry and the fire was crackling as Sally settled cross-legged in front of it and Maddy began to sketch.

"Do you see anything, Sally," she called out as she worked. Sally turned and looked at her. She had seen nothing in the fire, but now she thought she saw Tessa standing beside Maddy, smiling at her and running her hand over her long hair. She closed her eyes tightly and when she opened them, Maddy was alone on the porch.

"Well," Maddy said. "What did you see?"

Sally sighed and smiled. She never doubted that love lasted beyond the grave. She often felt the presence of her parents, especially when she was ill and needed reassurance. Sally's parents had died two years before within months of each other. She had been the child of a very late marriage. It did not seem strange that Tessa should come to this little party for Maddy.

"I didn't see anything in the fire, Maddy," she said truthfully. "Nothing at all."

The day Emily graduated from the little grade school

behind St. Mary's Church, she won the prize for being the best writer in the eighth grade. She stepped up to the stage to get a small blue ribbon with "excellence" stamped on it in gold letters. Daddy, Maddy, and Auntie Alice were sitting at the back of the room, applauding. As she walked to her seat, Em saw Al Kellogg, who helped her dad with the chores, smile at her from his place near the door. Her heart started to pound under the pale green, organdy dress Aunt Alice had bought for her in Indianapolis. Al had promised her a surprise, and she was excited because he knew what she wanted.

Her eyes caught Maddy's and she winked at her. At eleven, her sister was still a delicate child and her pink cheeks looked almost feverish. Em gestured toward Al and Maddy caught his eye and waved. Then everyone settled into the wooden folding chairs to hear Fr. Ryan's remarks. The pastor was a great favorite and loved to pepper his remarks with stories about individual students. Then it was time to award diplomas.

After the graduates received applause and filed out of the auditorium, the families followed, many stopping at Maddy's seat to say hello. After the last ones left, her daddy picked Maddy up and carried her to her chair in the hallway. She was light, and he lifted her with ease. She put her good arm around his neck and gave him a tight hug. Outside, in the warm June afternoon, under catalpas and maples and black walnut trees, the graduates stood in little knots of family and friends. Their teachers, Sisters of Providence, moved from group to group, talking and laughing, their black habits swinging as they walked.

When Emily was ready to go to the graduation party in the school library, her dad settled Maddy in the front seat of the car. "Don't stay too long, Em," Maddy called, poking her head out the window of the black Mercury. "I want to know what Al's giving you."

Em waved her fingers at Maddy, and then turned to find Opal. Her friend was standing at the door to the school, gesturing for her to hurry. On her shoulder was a little corsage of pink carnations. Opal was smiling broadly.

"Gene gave me flowers," she said, blushing a little. "Nan and Kelly are so green." Em leaned toward the flowers to catch their fresh scent.

"They're perfect on that dress, Opal. He sure has a case on you." As they walked in where the others were gathering, Eddie Gerard was standing in the hall, talking to Nan Erlander, his arm against the wall over her head. As Em walked by he looked up, his lips pursed in a wolf whistle. She gave him a weak smile and looked away. He shrugged and leaned down to say something to Nan, but his eyes were still following Em. Em felt her cheeks flush and hoped he didn't notice. She wondered what it would be like to put her fingers in his thick, curly hair and to stare into his hazel eyes. Every time he looked at her, she wondered what the girls meant when they said he was a bit wild. She knew he had kissed Nan breathless one evening at the May carnival. She was leaving the Ferris wheel with Opal when she saw them standing behind one of the stands where they had a hoop pitching game. Nan was looking up at him with a dazed expression in her brown eyes and one of his hands was on her breast. Emily had been startled when he raised his head and looked directly at her. He then dropped his hand and slowly, deliberately smiled at her. Opal thought he was the handsomest boy in the world and mooned over him. Emily stayed out of his way.

She looked quickly at Opal who was nudging her. "That Nan sure is fast." Opal let out a small sigh, not so much in disapproval as in envy, Emily thought.

"Oh, Opal," Emily said, "you've got to see what my dad gave me for graduation. It's a mirror that was made in Venice, Italy. It has the loveliest amethyst glass around its sides. Dad says he gave it to Mom for a wedding present and that she said it would go to their oldest girl one day. He said he was sure she would want me to have it now, as her graduation present to me.

It's hanging on the wall in my room and it shines like something out of a fairy tale." The girls walked to the small library where there were tables set with dishes of ice cream with canned peaches for sundaes and chocolate cookies as big as your hand.

Kendra Munro's dress was the prettiest. "My grandmother bought it on a trip to Chicago," she said proudly.

"Oh. I just love the way the white silk feels," said Opal. The dress, with its insets of lace and pink rosettes, made plain Kendra almost pretty. Her voice rose in a rare giggle of delight as the other girls admired it.

Alice Munro came into the library looking for Emily. She was holding a small white box. She drew her aside to a corner of the library filled with a tall palm.

"This is for you, Emily." Removing the blue silk ribbon around the box, Emily opened it to find one of the cherished gold lockets resting on a velvet pouch.

"Oh, Auntie Alice, I love it. Thank you so much. I can't believe you're giving it to me."

"Let me put it on, dear. Your mother would be so proud of you." As Emily pulled her hair up, Alice slipped the locket over her head and whispered. "I'll give the other locket on the chain to Maddy on her graduation. And my matching bracelet with the gold locket will go to the first of you two girls to become a mother."

The girls clustered around as Emily showed them the golden locket that glittered around her neck. Kendra's face became pale and she bit her lip in consternation. Only Billy Caine noticed. He pulled her aside. "Kendra, what's wrong?"

"That was supposed to be mine, Billy. She had no right." She turned away before he could see the tears in her eyes and walked out of the room. Billy followed her. He put his arm around her and talked to her until he made her smile. He never seemed to see that she wasn't pretty. He told her she had the whitest skin and the softest hands. Sometimes the only time she didn't feel sad was when she was with Billy. He could make her laugh. She didn't laugh often.

Em was restless, eager to show Maddy her wonderful gift. She wanted to leave, to walk home to her big white house on Woodlawn Street where Maddy would be on the swing waiting for her. She kissed Opal on the cheek, said her thanks to Sr. Evelyn, her eighth grade teacher, and walked quickly down the road toward home. Her dress felt gauzy against her legs and her heart was pounding.

Al wasn't there when she walked up the sidewalk to the porch. Maddy was settled in the swing with her drawing pad and pencils.

"Don't worry, Em, he's inside eating Aunt Alice's plum cake." Her eyes were teasing as they rested on her sister's face. When she saw the locket around Emily's neck, she put her small hand over her mouth in surprise.

"She gave it to me, Maddy. Auntie Alice gave it to me." As she saw the longing in her sister's eyes, she added, "She means to give you the other one when you graduate, but don't let on I told you. And that's not all. The first one of us to have a baby will get the little gold bracelet with the locket as her special gift." The two girls were laughing and hugging when Al came bursting through the screen door, his silver hair and beard brighter than ever against his tan skin.

"Well, gradjeeate, star English student, congratulations!"

Emily smiled. She didn't speak, just stood with her fingers holding the locket and looked at him quietly and intently.

"Okay, okay. Let's get on with this. Close your eyes and stay right here." When she thought she couldn't stand it another minute, Al said, "Open your eyes." She did.

"This is Bess, Em. Bess, this is Em." A small, red-tailed hawk was perched on his fist, her talons gripping his leather glove, her head turning sharply from side to side as each eye caught the girl in its bright circle. Al handed Em another glove almost like his, and as he had taught her, she slipped it on and placed her gloved fist just a bit higher than Al's. Bess hopped onto Em's glove. Em wound the jesse straps tied to its talons through two of her gloved fingers and the bird spread its wings, moving from foot to foot, setting the small bell attached to her tail tinkling.

Em walked out to the front yard and tossed the bird upward where it flew over their heads into the tallest of the sugar maples. She was trembling with happiness. The hawk was the part of her that could fly—the part of her that had been missing. She felt herself moving on its wings, and closed her eyes. Al gave her a little nudge, understanding what she was feeling, and gave her the pouch of bits of flesh he had been holding. She placed a piece on her fist, tapped it and held her glove up high. Bess made a little bobbing motion with her head and Em knew she was judging the distance to the glove. The hawk came back to her, almost weightless on the glove. With the meat in her beak Bess moved her wings into a mantling position to protect it.

"Oh, Al, she's beautiful." Al grinned at her, his lined, old face showing his pleasure. He blinked back the tears that threatened. Her mother had been kind to him when he was looking for work and had talked her husband into hiring him. He had tried to repay that kindness by giving this special gift to her daughter.

"I've been training her for you, Em. Now you can come with me when I fly Alexander." Al's red tailed hawk, Alexander, was big and swift. More than once she had seen him bring down a pheasant for Al's table. Though the bird had a strident voice, it was not a screamer. She had thought that Al might teach her to fly Alexander. She had never dreamed that she would have her own hawk!

Bess preened herself on her perch and Emily called to her from the kitchen window as she washed her mother's thin, Rosenthal plates. Emily admired them as they turned in her soapy hands. But even the delicate beauty of Tessa's china couldn't compare to Bess.

"Isn't she beautiful?" she said for the hundredth time to Maddy who was sewing the raveled edge of their one good tablecloth.

"She is," Maddy said. Her small, left hand moved nimbly with the stitches, as graceful and mobile as her legs were not. "When can I hold her?"

"Oh, Mad!" Em said. "Bess needs to get used to me first." Maddy's little mouth drooped and her eyes lost their hopeful expression." Emily dried her hands on the towel she had thrown over her shoulder, and lifted Maddy's chin until she was looking directly into her eyes.

"Give me two weeks, Mad, and I'll let you fly her! Just two weeks." The smile Em loved curved her sister's mouth. "Thank you, Em. Thank you!"

Emily knew their father would not approve, afraid that Bess would fly at Maddy and cause her to lose her balance and be upset from her chair. She wondered how to make him understand that Bess was easy to fly and anyway, Maddy's frail body held the spirit of an adventurer. If he only knew! Maddy wasn't the only one with secrets. Her face flushed as she dried the last glass and put it in the cupboard.

"Be right back, Maddy," she said as she stepped out onto the back stoop. She sat down on the first step, hugging her aloneness; her time to think about what happened last Friday. She could feel her heart beating faster. She cupped her face in her hands and stared into the trees where the wind made the leaves restless.

Last Friday had been one of those perfect summer days that make you glad you live on a farm in Indiana. She had rolled Maddy's chair down the cleared path alongside the bean field. When they came to Blue Creek, she had pushed Maddy under the branches of the big river birch while she stripped to her panties and camisole and waded into the deepest part of the creek.

The water came quickly past her waist and almost covered her shoulders. She walked to the rock where a ledge projected, making a good place to sit. Pulling herself up, she sat on the cold, smooth surface, squeezing the water out of the ends of her hair and feeling the cool flow of water around her knees.

"It's cold, Maddy, but it makes your blood run fast and gives you little shivers."

Watching her from the wheelchair, Maddy said, "Oh, how I wish I could just get up and come sit by you."

Emily stopped kicking at the water. "Sorry, honey, I'm not tall enough or strong enough to get you here safely."

"I am, Maddy. Hang on." With a shiver more of excitement than cold, Em saw Eddie Gerard walk out of the woods and, leaning down, pick Maddy up as easily as if she were a doll. He was tall, already his adult height, and generally conceded to be the strongest boy in the graduating glass.

"Yes," Em called. "Oh, yes, Eddie, bring her here." In several long but careful strides, Eddie brought Maddy to the rock and lifted her up beside Em. The hem of her dress was wet and her long, slim legs were dangling, moving in the creek water as if at Maddy's direction. Eddie looked at the girls intently. "You two are always together—like twins—guess you have to make your own kind of good times." Em flushed, thinking of how childish she must look.

"Thank you Eddie," Maddy said, reaching for him and kissing him lightly on the lips.

"How about that. You want to try?" he grinned at Emily.

She was suddenly aware of her small breasts outlined by the wet camisole and her heart that was beating too fast. Then, some part of her told her not to mind. "Thanks, Eddie, not this time. Want to swim a little before you take Maddy back?"

"For a small price," he said, and leaning forward, pulled her toward him and placed his full mouth on hers. She trembled as she felt herself falling into the softness of his kiss. Her heart began to pound and her insides felt as strange and prickly as they did on the first dive on the roller coaster at Conner Park. When he pulled away slowly, she didn't want the kiss to stop. He kept his face close to hers and she couldn't look at him.

"Don't worry, Eddie, I won't tell," Maddy said. "Nobody ever did such a nice thing for me except Em. She always does."

"I'll bet," Eddie said softly, his eyes brushing Em's as she looked up. He gave a soft whistle and shook his head as though putting a thought aside.

He dove for rocks that Maddy could see glinting on the bottom of the creek. "Tiger rocks," she called them because of their stripes. He caught a small, green frog for her and soon Em forgot her shyness and her first kiss, and they played like three children on a day stolen from school.

When Eddie had carried Maddy back to her chair, Emily toweled her legs and arms and dried her own hair. Holding the towel under her chin so that it covered her, she looked at him.

"Thanks, Eddie," she said, "it was fun for Maddy."

"Was it fun for you, Em?" he teased, kissing her cheek and pulling a damp thread of her hair around his finger. He looked at her until she felt her ears go hot and pink. "Anybody ever tell you that you have cat's eyes?" Then he smiled at her and walked back into the woods.

The girl straddled the horse, grimacing at the aching of her back and lower abdomen. The bleeding had begun in earnest early this morning, and she had reconsidered running in the race. Opal knew she was the fastest rider among all the girls, and now, she thought, with a sinking feeling, she was the fastest girl, period. Lucky, too, she thought. The blood that drained from her body meant she had gambled and won.

A half-hearted smile touched the corners of her narrow lips. She had wanted Eddie ever since she was old enough to notice a boy. He was broad-shouldered, with a slim, hard body and curly brown hair that gleamed red in the sun.

"All the girls are crazy about him, but I'm the one he's taking to Senior Dance," she thought happily. She had wanted him to ask her and had given up hope. He used to tease her when he caught her watching him in class.

"Wistful little Opal," he called her, making her feel small and miserable. Then Nan Erlanger, the girl he spent most of his time with, moved out of town when her father got a new assignment with the railroad. Opal remembered Nan's tear-streaked face at the train window when the whole gang went to say goodbye. She was looking for Eddie, but, of course, he couldn't come. Nan's father hated Eddie and some said he moved his family because Nan wouldn't stop seeing him. Eddie told her that himself. She wondered why he wasn't more upset.

"Opal, he wants her to marry a college boy," Eddie had said. "Oh, well," he turned his hypnotic eyes on her face. "Guess I'll have to take somebody else to Senior Dance." She guessed she blushed, because he put his finger under her chin and asked if they were having a heat wave.

Every night for a week, they spent time together. He took her for a coke after school on Tuesday, met her at the library on Wednesday, and on Thursday afternoon, they played hooky and went to the Era Theater to see "The Three Musketeers." When she cried because the countess killed June Allyson, he put his arm around her and nuzzled her neck in sympathy. A chill shot through her body from the point where his lips touched her. He felt her stiffen and took her chin in his hand to turn her face toward him. There, in the top row of an almost empty balcony, he kissed her. When she caught her breath, she kissed him back.

There was more kissing in the car, and then he told her she was driving him crazy and that he needed her. He said they could go to his uncle's old barn on the back acreage of his place. He knew it was vacant, and they could have it all to themselves. When she pulled away and said she couldn't do that, he leaned back into the seat and was silent.

"Well, say something," she blurted out miserably, unable to bear the long, cold stare.

"I must have made a mistake. I thought you really wanted to be with me. Now I see all you really are is a girl who gets her kicks from teasing guys. I thought you liked me. Could have fooled me with all those cow eyes you were making."

"But I do like you. I like you more than anybody."

"But not enough to be my girl, right? Not enough to prove you want to be only my girl. It's not like I think you should be with any guy. Just me. I thought you were going to be my only girl, the girl I want to take to Senior Dance," he said softly.

"Your only girl?" She thought about walking into the gym with him on Senior Night, the pride she would feel when he put his arm around her and held her close when they danced. "You know I've never done it with anybody. Pastor Reid says that should be kept for marriage."

He leaned forward and looked earnestly into her eyes. "Opal, I know this would be your first time. That would make it so special between us. I know you're not the kind of girl who goes from guy to guy. Don't worry about not doing it before marriage. It doesn't matter. You'll be my one and only girl. Will you be my girl?" He leaned forward again and kissed her chin, her throat and suddenly Opal's lips found his.

Forever, she thought as she moved into the wave that was sweeping her away. I'll be your girl forever.

So they spent an hour at the barn. She hadn't known that Eddie would hurt her the first time. He told her she was beautiful and that she did it just right, but although the kissing made her feel good, the rest hurt. She told herself that the important thing was that Eddie enjoyed it, so she lied and told him it felt good to her. She knew she might get pregnant, but then he would marry her in the Liberty Baptist church where she had gone to Sunday school. She was just making love before the wedding instead of waiting until after.

Now, she thought, shivering with delight, I'll be going

with him to Senior Dance tomorrow night and everyone will know about us. It had to show. She felt so changed.

I'm the girl he loves. She hadn't told anyone about the barn, not even her best friend, Em. Tomorrow night they'd see for themselves. First, though, she had to win the girls' two miler. The senior girls' horse race was a tradition at Hawks Crossing High School. Her horse, Stoney, was unbeatable. Like me, she thought. Winning the race today, dancing with Eddie tomorrow. Will he ask me to marry him at the dance, or afterward in the barn? It didn't matter. Well, maybe it did. She wanted him to ask her now. She didn't want him to feel he had to ask her because she was in trouble.

Stoney shied at a small rabbit that jumped from the bushes. He was a bit skittish whenever she rode him at her time of the month. Maybe he could smell the blood because he was harder to control and seemed almost afraid.

Twenty riders in bright blouses and blue jeans clustered around the huge oak in front of the high school. Some of the girls had their hair tied back with scarves. Emily had pulled hers back into a ponytail like Opal's. When she rode up, a few of her friends called to her and waved. Em rode over to join them, then dismounted and held Lolly's nose against her neck. Named after her mother's mare, Lolly was willing, but Em knew she couldn't run with Stoney.

Em always looked vivid, Opal thought, because of her red hair and creamy skin. Today, the cool air had brought the color to her cheeks and her green eyes glowed, but for the first time, Opal didn't envy Em's looks. Eddie preferred soft brown hair and big brown eyes.

"This isn't fair, Opal, no one can beat Stoney. My old Lolly won't even try," she laughed. Em looked at her friend thoughtfully. Opal was more animated lately and even though she was not a pretty girl, her expression and the shining happiness in her eyes made her striking. She had seen her with Eddie a few times. Maybe that was the answer.

After Nan left, Emily had daydreamed that Eddie would walk up to her after English class, lean against her locker and ask her if he could drive her home. But it was Opal Eddie chose.

"Hey, Opal, let's see my best girl win." Eddie walked up to them smiling at Opal and teasing Em with a long stare that took her in from her boots to the ribbon in her hair. Em turned away before he could see the blush coloring her throat and cheeks.

"How's Bess, Em? Ever going to let me fly her?" Eddie asked. Emily shook her head.

"Al says for now only I should hunt with her. He's teaching me how to handle hawks. There's a lot to learn."

He looked at her the way he had the afternoon she still remembered, the afternoon he'd kissed her. "That's true about a lot of things, Em."

The girls lined up and a crowd of parents, kid brothers and sisters, and boyfriends shouted encouragement. It was a tradition, this race to Kelly's Bridge and back. The girl who won became queen of the Senior Dance and crowned her escort king. The girls of Hawks Crossing High School were good riders and the race was one of the best events of senior week.

Stoney stamped and snorted but Opal spoke soothing words into the erect, shapely ear, and he quieted. Kenneth Munro, the principal, raised a flag in his right hand, and grinned at his daughter Kendra who sat nervously atop her horse.

"Ready ladies? Watch the flag and when it drops on the count of three, you're off." The red flag fell, causing a burst of cheering from the crowd and suddenly the girls were racing toward the bridge, leaving a small dust storm behind them. Opal leaned forward, her head against Stoney's neck. He seemed to fly just above ground. She was already leading the others, and approaching a small knot of river birches. A flash of red, like Em's hair, she thought later, shot between Stoney's hooves. In the space between heartbeats, she was on the ground; face down, with a shattering sensation of pain in her right ankle. She held her breath in agony and then was swallowed by a black cloud.

The emergency room nurse was checking her blood pressure when Opal woke to the grip of pain in her right ankle and foot. She moaned and the nurse's eyes flashed to her face. It was Mrs. Wilson, whose brother lived on the farm next to Opal's family's place.

She brought two pills and a glass of water to Opal. "Doc Reuter said to give you these when you woke if the pain is bad."

Opal reached for the pills in the small paper cup. "It's bad, Mrs. Wilson," she said. "Did I break it?"

"Doc had some X-rays done. He'll be in to talk to you as soon as he reads them. As she turned away she said, "Your Dad's here. Do you want me to let him in now?"

"Sure." She leaned back into the pillows, her eyes beginning to burn. Instead of dancing with Eddie tomorrow night at the Senior Dance, she'd be talking to her father. The idea hit her suddenly and she let the tears come. She didn't want to see her father. She wanted Eddie. Where was he?

Opal's father, tall and thin-faced with the small eyes his daughter had inherited, came into the room in his usual deferential way. He looked at her with a mix of love and worry. He didn't understand his daughter. He had tried to fill her life, but he had failed. All she had ever really wanted was the quiet, discontented woman who kept to herself until the day she left her husband and daughter and ran off with a man from the nearby town of English.

"I'm okay, Dad. Don't look so fussed." She glared at him through her pain. Why did he always look like that, worried and afraid? Why couldn't he forget her mother? She had learned that the trick was to let herself get angry and then it didn't hurt so much. Calvin smiled and she relented. He really did love her. "I'm okay, Dad," she said, holding out her arms. Her father smiled and some of the anxious lines disappeared around his eyes as he hugged his daughter.

Eddie did come to see Opal in the early evening. He looked around, obviously uncomfortable as he stood beside her bed.

"Hi, Opal, how are you?" She reached for him and he leaned over her carefully, planting a gentle kiss on her forehead.

"It's my ankle that's the problem, not my mouth, Eddie." Pulling him closer, she kissed him long and hard.

"Girl, you're giving me ideas." She flushed with pleasure.

"I'm sorry, Eddie, I really am. I'd do anything to change what happened. I'm so sorry we won't make the dance."

"Yeah, what am I gonna do while they keep you here? Hospitals give me the willies. You don't want me to stay here if it drives me crazy, do you?"

"Yes," she wanted to scream. "I do want you here. I hurt and I need you." Something told her not to say it out loud.

"Who sent the flowers?"

"Gene sent them. He said he'd stop by later." She and Gene had been in kindergarten together. He was sweet on her and she knew he always would be.

She saw the look in Eddie's eyes. "Isn't Gene taking Emily to the dance?" She nodded.

"Well that's it, girl. They're just friends. If he's sending you flowers, he would probably prefer to be here with you than at prom night. Of course, it would be a shame for Em to miss the dance because Gene's with you. Probably would be nice of me to take her." He had the sense to look a bit sheepish at the suggestion.

Her heart hurt inside her chest. She took a deep breath and admitted that Eddie would never be the man she had hoped he would be. But he was the one she wanted and whatever he needed, she would try to see he had. She had to admit that what she gave him was a release for his physical desires. He never spent much time talking with her or making plans. Anyway, taking Em to the Senior Dance would give her no worries. Em would never go to the barn, she admitted to herself.

Later that night Gene poked his head into her room. His face was very tan and his smile was sweet and slow. Why did she never want to run her fingers through his hair or kiss that smiling mouth? Sometimes she caught herself wishing she could, but he was more like a brother than a friend. She sighed and held out her hand.

"Come in, Gene. Thanks so much for the flowers." His grin grew wider and he looked down at her as though she was the most desirable girl in the world. Unlike Eddie, he seemed relaxed in the hospital room. His big frame was comforting and so was the look in his eyes. For a moment she thought of Emily and realized that even Em with her beauty couldn't make Gene look at her that way. Em hadn't been the one who spent those evenings in the barn with Eddie either. For the first time in her life, Opal Bauer felt beautiful and felt the power of beauty.

"Gene," she said softly, "I want to ask you a really big favor. I haven't been resting too well lately and Doc says I need somebody around to distract me from the pain in my ankle. I know you're planning to take Em to the Senior Dance, but I wondered if you could change your plans and stay with me tomorrow evening."

Gene's eyes lit up like a high voltage wire had been run through him. "Of course I would. I'd love too." His smile faded a moment. "What about Eddie?"

So, she thought, it wasn't such a secret. "Oh Eddie hates hospitals. It drives him crazy to sit here very long," she said truthfully. She ignored the look of disgust that was in his eyes. "Do you think Em would mind if Eddie took her to the dance instead?"

Gene looked at her thoughtfully for a moment and looked as though he wanted to say something. Then he smiled again and took her hand. "I'll ask her. We're not going steady or anything. We're just good friends. She's your friend, too, Opal, I'll ask her."

Emily still couldn't believe her luck. She shivered at the thought of being Eddie's date. Standing in front of the long mirror in her parent's room, she fastened her gold clip earrings and checked the hem of her waltz length blue dress. Sally had taken some classes in hairdressing, and she had pulled Em's hair into a French twist with tendrils at her temples and forehead. The dress was simple and she could feel the skirt against her legs when she moved. She wore the gold locket Aunt Alice had given her when she graduated from eighth grade. Her class ring was on her finger but she left her brown, rounded arms bare.

She closed her eyes and dabbed some Shalimar, another gift from Aunt Alice, behind her ears, on the nape of her neck and the crook of her arms. With a grin, she put two drops behind her knees. Standing close to the mirror, she studied her face. The light make up, rosy lipstick and eyeliner made her look a bit like a stranger. She was a somewhat glamorous Emily. Would Eddie think so? She knew she was only a substitute for Opal tonight, but she was excited at the idea of feeling Eddie's arms around her as they danced and listening to his voice. Looking into his eyes was a pleasure she had only daydreamed about. She wondered if he still remembered that day at Blue Creek when he had kissed her.

Even if it were just for one night, Eddie would be her date and when he brought her home . . . her heart was pounding. And when he brought her home, he would kiss her again, the way he had at the creek four years earlier.

As for Gene, she smiled as she thought of him with Opal. He was bringing her a corsage to wear on her robe and he would be having a supper tray in her room. He was so excited. He had always loved Opal for reasons beyond Emily's comprehension.

Although she was her oldest friend, Em knew all of Opal's faults. She wasn't pretty, certainly, but she did have a full, round figure. She always seemed to want the things she couldn't have, and was never satisfied with the good things that came to her, like Gene's love. She could be selfish and even cruel, and sometimes she grew angry at Em for no reason at all.

After Eddie pinned her corsage on the shoulder of her dress, and her parents took some pictures, they stepped out onto the porch into the warm evening air. Eddie took a deep breath. "Isn't it a great evening, Em?" She looked at him in a kind of wonder. He was startlingly handsome in his tuxedo. He looked like a movie star, she thought. He didn't miss her appreciative glances. His lips were close to her ear as he told her how lovely she looked and with his right hand tight around her, he guided her down the steps. The sensation where his hand curved around her waist made her aware of her body in a way she had never felt before.

The dance in the school gym was in full swing when they arrived. Walking beside Eddie as they crossed the dance floor, Em could feel the eyes of the other girls and she heard a few exclamations of surprise. Eddie was a good dancer and soon he was holding her against him. She breathed in his aftershave and leaned into the curve of his face and neck. At one point, he put their joined hands behind his back and held her closer. They didn't talk about Opal and Gene.

"Look at me, sunshine." She found herself losing all sense of time and place as she swam in his disturbing gaze. She pulled away from him a bit, embarrassed at the touch of his body, but he pulled her close. "Just relax, Em, don't be so nervous." His voice was soft, pleading with no teasing in it.

After the senior president crowned them King and Queen everyone applauded and Eddie led her down the steps from the stage to the dance floor. She felt it happen. She knew exactly when it happened. Eddie was so handsome and he felt so good in her arms that Em fell hopelessly in love with him while the band played the Queen's Dance music, the song Opal had chosen, "Blue Moon."

Afterward they went to a party at Kendra Munro's home. Diane Munro, wearing a frilled apron, served breakfast at about five A.M. and the night ended. In front of her house, Eddie stopped the car and turned off the engine. He looked at Em for a long time. "Are you memorizing my face, Eddie, since we aren't going to go out together anymore?"

"What? Why? Don't you want to go out again?" he asked in a soft, almost unrecognizable voice.

"You're Opal's boyfriend, so I guess the answer is no."

"But if I weren't? Would you want to see me again?"

She didn't answer for a long time. He smiled and leaned over to kiss her cheek, her neck, and then her mouth. The kiss was lingering. It was a promise, or maybe, she thought, a temptation.

"I want to see you again, too. Very much." He put his finger under her chin and looked into her eyes. "Em, you're too good for the likes of me. I've known it all along and tried to keep out of your way. But I can't. I want to see you. Don't be afraid, I'll never hurt you." He kissed her again but when she tightened her arms around him, her mouth opening under his, he moved her away from him. "I'll call you tomorrow," he said. For one awful moment, she wondered if he was only teasing her, but his eyes lingered on her face and there was no laughter in them.

The rest of that hot July and August, while Opal struggled with therapy, it was Gene who was always there to take her to her appointments. Eddie took Emily out to Stamper Creek for picnics, and they wandered through the caves and found the remnants of an Indian village. He even went with her to the small Catholic Church on Sundays. But Opal knew that he never took her to the barn.

Once, after Opal was home and her folks were visiting her aunt in Indianapolis, he came to the house and they made love. She was afraid he only wanted her because he couldn't ask

Emily to give him the physical pleasure he craved. He called her less and less often and didn't stay long when he came. She was frantic to keep him near her and would agree to lovemaking anytime he wanted it. But he didn't seem to want it anymore.

She remembered the day in September when he came for the last time. Sunlight was shining on the billowing leaves of the poplar trees in her yard. It was a cool, clear day that made her think about the coming hayrides and steaming chili afterward. She was completely happy, probably for the last time in her life.

"Opal, I have something I have to tell you. I've been seeing Emily for a long time. I don't know exactly how it happened but I love her and I'm going to ask her to marry me. We've been great friends, Opal, and I hope you'll be happy for me."

His eyes were wide and he looked directly at her. His words had come out in a rush and he was clearly relieved. He really saw no reason for her not to be happy for him.

"Great friends? You and Emily? I thought you loved me. All those times we were together?"

His face changed and he didn't look at her. "All those times were great. We gave each other lots of good times, lots of pleasure," She began to feel sick. "But there was never any question of our getting married. I never said anything about that, Opal."

She thought she was going to faint. Hold on, she told herself, don't look like a fool. "No, you never did, but then why did you, I mean why did we . . . "

"We were just having fun. You did have fun didn't you?"

She looked up at him with all her heart in her eyes. "Don't do this, Opal," he said in an angry voice that frightened her. She had never been frightened of him before. "I taught you some things you didn't know. Teach them to Gene."

She watched him leave the yard. Getting up with the help of her crutches, she went back into the house. The pain of disappointment was so deep she could hardly breathe. She got back to her bedroom and sat down heavily in the rocker beside her small chest. On top was a picture of herself and Eddie taken before the accident. She turned it face down. Beside it was a stack of senior pictures. She flipped through the small smiling faces until she found Emily's. Try as she might, she just couldn't hate Eddie. But she could hate the girl who took him away from her. Slowly and deliberately, with tears in her eyes and a heart as numb as ice, she tore the picture into small pieces.

Eddie and Emily married that November in St. Michael's Church. Gene had slipped a gold band on Opal's finger in Crown Point, Indiana earlier that same month.

Before Eddie's wedding, Opal rode Stoney to the barn. She walked in and looked around for a long time. "I can always come here when I want to remember," she said, her hand on the soft swell of her stomach. Overhead a hawk screamed and the skies began to darken with the promise of a cold winter.

Maddy's Journal

I never thought I'd have my own love story to tell. But I do, and I'm writing it here so that someday my daughter may read it and understand that life is a mystery and love is its answer.

My sister Em is a big part of my story, but then she always has been at the heart of my life. After she married Eddie we spent less time together because Eddie took all of her time. He couldn't get enough of being with her. I remember that he flirted with lots of girls when they were in high school, but once my Em loved him and married him, he never seemed to notice any other girl. One humid night, when my window was open, I heard Eddie telling her she was the only person he had ever really loved and that he would always try to make her happy. He promised her over and over that nothing else and no one else would ever come between them. I had never heard him speak that way, so intensely, almost fiercely.

A year after their wedding, Edward took Em to meet his grandmother, his mother's mother, who had been sick with influenza the day of the ceremony. They asked me to go with them. I almost decided not to go. I almost missed the most important trip of my life.

We stayed at Edward's grandmother's house just outside Louisville. I was tired from the drive and yet all my senses were stimulated. The green hills of southern Indiana gave way to the bridge over the Ohio and then to dusty roads that led to a rocky creek and a farmhouse with a lovely porch wrapped around it. A large, red dog ran barking alongside the car.

"Cinnamon!" The Golden Retriever stopped its forward run and, tongue hanging, trotted back toward the old woman who called him from the steps. She came toward us, arms outstretched, the dog at her side.

"Edward!" Her dark eyes were shiny with tears. He dropped the luggage and held out his arms as he moved toward her. For a moment, Em felt a stab of envy at the way they greeted each other. Then Edward gave his hand to Em and tugged her forward. "What do you think of her, Gran? Isn't she everything I promised?" Edward's arm moved around Em's shoulders and pulled her close. "And more," his grandmother agreed, the slightest burring of her "r" betraying her Scottish origins. "Your hair is the color of the fox, Emily. You are a beauty." She kissed Em's cheek. Small and frail with salt and pepper hair, her skin had a scrubbed look that reflected light and made her seem younger than her years. Then Em walked with her to the car so that she could introduce me. I liked the way Anne McFarland's brown eyes met mine in warmth and pleasure. She would not mind that my legs were not strong enough to carry me. I was sure that she was not the kind who offered pity instead of friendship, and I could tell she liked what she saw in my face. Sometimes you meet someone and know that you are discovering an old friend. She put her warm cheek against mine.

"Girl," she said, "you are as welcome as cider at a picnic," and I heard her throaty laugh for the first time. It sounded a lot like Eddie's. When Eddie came back from the house where he had taken our suitcases, he opened the door and reached for me with his usual grin.

"Come on, you, and I hope you haven't gained a pound on the trip." I knew why my sister loved him. Eddie was always teasing, always made you see how bright and new the light was around you, how full of opportunity each day was. He lifted me with ease. As he carried me toward the house, I saw that a man stood in the doorway. He was a large man with a dark beard, and he was wiping his hands with a paint-spattered rag. He must have watched us greet each other. The man smiled directly at me. His eyes were so brown as to be almost black. His mouth changed and only a shadow of the smile remained. Eddie greeted him and Gran waved her hand in his direction. "Everyone, this is Fredryk Bauer. Fredryk this is my grandson Edward, his wife Emily, and her sister Madeleine. Fredryk is visiting me. He is the only son of my best friend Karen, gone now these many years. Come, Fredryk, and say hello."

He took the steps down two at a time, held out a large, brown hand to Edward and nodded to me without speaking. It was not a greeting; it was a gesture of recognition. Although he didn't touch me, I knew his hand would feel warm, enveloping, and possessive. I couldn't look away. "I'll help with your bags," he said to Eddie. Eddie's grandmother put her arm around Em's waist and pulled her toward the porch.

We drank coffee at the large, oak table in Gran's kitchen. There was chicken in the oven, almost ready, and an apple pie with a sugared crust waited on the sideboard. Eddie talked about family with his grandmother and about his plans to continue living in Hawks Crossing.

"Hawks Crossing?" Fredryk repeated the name of the town with interest. "Isn't that an odd name for a town?" Eddie smiled. "I guess so. But it's where we were born and where we hope to stay." Em then spoke softly for the first time, "It's an old Indiana town settled by some families who brought falcons here and caught and trained some local birds." Anne's eyes twinkled. "Don't look so surprised, Fredryk, other people fly hawks, too."

"You have a hawk?" Em asked, her eyes shining.

"I had one. I bought him from an old man in Kentucky. I don't call him anymore. I let him go, not that he wanted to, lazy thing. He preferred to be fed!" Em's face became remarkable when she laughed. I thought she must be the most beautiful girl in Indiana. I wanted Fredryk to look at me but why would he do that when he could look at Em?

Later, as we drank iced tea on the porch, Fredryk sat on the corner railing where the shadows deepened around him. My heart began to pound because I could tell that he was watching me with his smoky, golden eyes.

"You know, my dear, I think you should sleep in tomorrow morning," Edward's grandmother's voice broke in on my thoughts. "Emily, Edward, and I will have to leave early and, of course, Fredryk will go very early to catch the sunrise on his canvas. I'll leave some chicken and salad for your lunch, and we should be home by ten. Would you mind my dear? It would mean so much for my brother to meet Emily, and I'm afraid that it would be a very uncomfortable trip for you on some rough roads." I remember thinking that I would be alone with Fredryk all day if they went without me. I warmed at the idea.

"Yes, of course. Do go without me. I'll be fine. If Fredryk doesn't mind carrying me out to the porch, I can spend the day doing some needlepoint and reading." I was too shy to draw in the presence of a real artist. "Perhaps I'll watch him paint, if he doesn't mind doing some sketching on the porch before he goes out into the fields."

From a corner of the porch, she could barely hear his answer. "No trouble at all."

"What's this?" Gran seemed surprised and gave us the gift of her laugh. "I've never known you to welcome someone observing you while you're working. Well. This is definitely an improvement. Thank you, Maddy, we may even get a better look at what our mysterious painter is doing."

Em settled me in the bedroom off the kitchen and then went upstairs to the bedroom Gran said had once been her nursery. Gran would sleep in her sewing room so that Edward and Emily could share the larger room. Fredryk had his quarters above the barn where the hired hands used to sleep. After they went to bed, I lay awake a long time, staring at the flowered wallpaper reflected in the glow of the bedside lamp. Each time I moved, the springs creaked and my restlessness caused me to move often. As I made myself more comfortable, I wondered about Fredryk, who he was and why he was here. And most of all, I wondered why the look in his eyes stayed with me in the night and why I wasn't thinking of myself as a lame woman but someone young and pretty. As I turned in the bed to reach for my sketch pad on the table beside it, the springs in the old bed creaked again. I heard a slight tap on my door.

"I thought I heard you moving around," Fredryk said, standing in the doorway, after I had called out "Come in." "If you are too warm, I'll be glad to open the window." His deep voice was slightly accented. I hadn't noticed that before.

"No, it's fine," I answered, "but I really would like to go back to the kitchen for awhile. Would you mind? It's cooler." Somehow, I was sure he had been sitting there, smoking and sketching at the round oak table. I reached for my robe, which was on the chair near the bed, and then as he bent down, I wound my stronger arm around his neck. He lifted me as if I was precious, breakable, and light as a feather. My heart raced as my weight settled against his chest. I remembered when Eddie carried me into the creek to the rock where Em was sitting. Even then, I felt that something strange had happened. Now I knew it had foreshadowed this moment. I was startled by my desire to bury my face in Fredryk's neck. He carried me to the padded armchair at the side of the table nearest the window in the kitchen. My feet were bare and I was glad that they were small and perfectly formed, even though my legs were weak and couldn't bear my weight. He picked up the pad in front of the chair where he had been sitting and began making short, quick strokes with is pencil.

"You couldn't sleep either," he said without looking up.

"I guess I couldn't. It's too warm."

"Yes, warm," he said, still not lifting his eyes from the sheet. I asked him what he was drawing.

"Just making a small sketch." He handed me the pad. There, in a beautiful, soft rendering was my face, only the expression on it was much lovelier than anything I had ever seen in the mirror. I looked at it a moment, then, realizing I was holding my breath, I glanced up at his face. Those warm, golden eyes were full on my face, and I felt their gaze like a caress.

"Don't you like it?" he asked.

"Well, it's beautiful," I said, "but truthfully I don't think it's really me."

His laugh was deep. "Oh, it's you all right, Maddy. May I call you Maddy?" The sound of his voice saying my name sent a shiver along my arms.

"Why did you laugh?" I asked.

"I don't think you know yourself very well. This is very definitely you. May I get you some lemonade?" He went to the white cabinet to get two glasses, opened the refrigerator, and poured the pale liquid over ice. I could hear the ice cubes clinking. We drank the lemonade and then he carried me back to bed and said goodnight. Before he shut the door he said, "It should have been wine," laughed, and left as though nothing at all had happened.

Early the next morning, Fredryk carried me to the side of a creek where he had been painting. He had already carried a porch chair to the place, and placed me gently on the blanket with which he had covered it. Then he raised my legs gently to the stool and smiled at me. Not a word, just that slow, knowing smile. Then he went to the canvas and worked until lunchtime. For a long while I just watched him, but I fell asleep, probably because I had been unable to sleep much of the night.

I felt so refreshed when I woke that it was a moment before I realized I was still not in the bedroom off the kitchen. A fine rain was falling and I was reclining most comfortably on a chair. Fredryk was standing looking down at me, his arms outstretched.

"Wake up Sleeping Beauty and let me get you to some shelter before you are soaked." He lifted me easily and for a moment before he moved, he pressed his face against my cheek. "You smell like lilacs," he said. I remember thinking I must thank Em for the lilac dusting powder she gave me for my last birthday. He moved into the trees and where the leaves formed a heavy canopy, he sat carefully on the ground, cradling me gently. I had never been so happy as that afternoon, warm in his arms, listening to the sound of the rain on the leaves. When he bent down to meet my eyes, I felt the beating of my heart. It began to pound harder and harder as he kissed me. As we kissed each other.

"I hardly know you, Fredryk," I said touching his face. "So why do I feel like I know you better than anyone else?" He looked at me again with that same intense glow in his eyes.

"All you need to know, you know, Madeleine." The expression in his eyes changed and he turned away from me into silence.

I knew then, without asking him. I had found my love, but as surely as if he had told me, I knew that another woman had loved him first. She was not just a woman from whom he could walk away; she was a woman to whom he had committed himself. I looked at my poor weak legs that prevented me from running away from this awful moment, those legs that named me an invalid, a woman most men would not have the courage to love. They had not mattered to Fredryk.

I turned his face back to me. "You are leaving aren't you, Fredryk?"

His eyes were wet with tears and despairing. "Yes. Before I hurt my wife and my children. I am not free." He looked at me intently. "I think you know that."

We looked at each other across the chasm that separated us. I believed that he was my only chance for happiness, for completeness, and though it was wrong, I would be with him once, before we let each other go.

"They will be back late tonight. We have only hours to be together. Love me, Fredryk, for if you don't, how can I face the rest of my life without you?" We went back to the house, the rain leaving its tears on our faces. I cannot write of those hours. There are no words.

I am filled with excitement but I must plan carefully. My child and Em's child will be born about the same time. Fredryk's child will bring new meaning into my life. I have decided to tell the family that I am going to a clinic in Chicago to seek relief from the pain in my legs. I have already written to St. Elizabeth's Home in Indianapolis. There, women like me have their babies and decide what they will do next. I know what I will do, of course. I will find a way to keep our child and to raise her. For the first time since Fredryk left, I feel the joy of living. I ask God to forgive me, to forgive us both, and to grant me a safe delivery and health to the child. He is merciful and I have sought his forgiveness in the darkness of the confessional. I am unafraid and sure his hand will guide me.

The child has been born and I have named her Delores, because she is the child of my sad love. I am not recovering as well as I should be and often I feel weak and feverish. My greatest joy is when I nurse her, pressing her tiny, perfect body to mine. Lately I have been dreaming of the house where I was born and the mother I only know from pictures. Last night she came to me in a dream, held me in her arms, and whispered to me in the language of her childhood. I felt comforted and happy when I awoke. My nurse, Judith Kelley, is a gentle woman who can never have a child. I asked her to raise my Delores if anything should happen to me. She cried when I asked her and told me that I would live to raise the child myself, but we both knew the truth. She has promised and I am content. Fredryk would like her. She will be good to our child. How I long to ask Em to take her, but she still lives in our old world and I cannot send my child there to pay the price of her mother's great, but unlawful love. Ah, Em, how I wish I could see you one more time. My sister, how I love you! You were my hope, my legs, and my freedom when I was a child. Sister, mother, and friend, you have been all three. Remember me and pray for my soul. God is merciful. I thank him for my beautiful life. Our mother did not leave the world to birth a puny life. I could not run with my legs, so I ran with my spirit. As Em flew her Bess, I, too, have flown the wild hawk of Joy. Mother, thank you for buying my happiness with your very life. Soon, very soon, I will see you and I will embrace you and thank you.

Kyle

Edward drove his truck into the gravel area at the side of Gene's barn. He was particular about returning tools as quickly as possible and it would give him a chance to spend time with Kyle and Greg.

"Hello, Mr. Gerard!" The blonde head of the younger son, Greg, came into sight as the boy came out of the barn. He had straw on his shirt and was slapping the dirt off his hands. The youngster's broad grin, very much like Gene's, widened further as Edward opened the door and tossed him the keys.

"Hi, Greg. Will you help me get this sharpening wheel out of the truck and then drive it over to your woodpile? I need another load of firewood, too. No sassafras, now. Don't need any bad luck." Greg grinned.

He walked toward the house after watching Greg drive away with a smooth motion. Edward shook his head appreciatively. The boy was a natural with all kinds of machinery and with people, too.

Opal came to the door as he stepped onto the porch. "Morning," he said, and she pushed the door open with a smile and a slight flush.

"Sit down and have some fresh coffee." She filled a cup with the dark liquid and placed it in front of him on the Formica table she had covered with a plastic tablecloth.

Edward looked around the kitchen as he sipped the strong coffee. Unlike Emily's kitchen which was simple and light-filled, Opal's kitchen was cluttered with bottles, cooking utensils, bowls, and dishes of assorted patterns. Some were chipped, old bowls she was apparently reluctant to discard. The kitchen was clean but dull in comparison to Em's yellow walls, blue china, and flowers on the polished wooden table.

Opal sat opposite him, twisting her wedding ring with her right hand and watching him.

"Gene and Kyle went to get the new rifle we promised him for his birthday. They won't be back for a little while."

"The boy is good with guns," Edward said, nodding in agreement to his own observation. "Gene has two fine sons, Opal. You've made him a happy man."

Her pale eyes held his for a moment, until he dropped his. "Have you missed not having a son?" she asked. He hoped he had only imagined a hint of a smile at the corner of her lips which had grown thinner with time.

"Every man would like to have a son," he said, and then quickly added as if in Emily's defense, "but Jessie and Elizabeth are the light of my eyes."

Opal continued to stare at him and Edward became uncomfortable. She never spoke of it, but when she looked at him that way, he knew she was thinking of the time they had shared their bodies so carelessly when they were very young. He hated that look. It reminded him of the boy he had been, hedonistic, and unable to handle his sexuality. He was not proud of those days. Except when he was near Opal, he never thought of them. Em had changed his life so completely. Usually the insinuating look in Opal's eyes disappeared when he began to talk about Emily. Her name was something he evoked as an antidote to Opal's memories.

"Emily is teaching the girls how to fly Bess. They love the way Bess comes to her whistle. I swear they think she is a magical princess with special powers. Actually," he laughed softly, "she is!" He glanced at Opal only to find the look he feared still in her eyes. For some reason, he felt a tightening in his chest and a desire to walk out of her kitchen as quickly as possible. Something dangerous was rising in those eyes, a tide that even Emily's name couldn't stem.

"Eddie," her voice was soft and a little breathless, "Eddie, do you remember where we were fifteen years ago?" He looked at her with surprise. "No, of course not, Opal. Who could remember after that many years?" He laughed and her chin came up. She looked at him directly. "I can. I know exactly where we were, Eddie."

"Opal, I'm not good at games." He started to go. "Thanks for the coffee, but I have to leave. Tell Gene I'll . . ."

"Wait, Eddie." She rose and put her fingers on his arm. She tightened them. "Listen, I have something important to say to you." Her face reddened and she breathed quickly. For a moment, he thought she was ill.

"All right, Opal. What is it?" He sat down again. She remained standing stiffly.

"Fifteen years ago," she said deliberately in a hoarse whisper, "we were in your uncle's barn and you were in such a hurry that we made love on the ground." She put her hand tightly across his mouth as he started to speak. "Don't you know, Eddie? Don't you really know that Kyle is your son? Didn't you know I married Gene because I was pregnant?"

His mind swallowed her words and he sat quietly for a moment, stunned at his elation. Not shame or fear, but elation. Aware of the excitement in his body as he thought of Kyle, he repeated her words, "My son. Kyle is my son." A sudden weight dragged down his spirit. "Does Gene know?"

Opal felt her body warm with triumph. He never doubted her for a moment. She sat down quickly and took his hand in her own shaking ones. "No, no, of course not. He thinks the boy is his. Look at him, Eddie. You can see it if you look." She reached up and touched his hair, the same hair as Kyle's. Her fingers tingled as she laid both hands on the table.

"My dear God, Opal." He put his head down on her hands and she closed her eyes, emptied for once of all the envy that had been building over the years. She was again the center of Eddie's thoughts and Eddie's touch. Right then he was hers and not Emily's.

When he raised his head, he met her eyes and smiled. "He's wonderful, Opal. Is he really mine?" She shook her head, her eyes filled with tears, knowing he knew she was telling the truth, wanting only to hear it again.

She took her time and squeezing his hands, she shared his elation. Then she told him her secret. She told him what would bind them together for the rest of their lives. "I told him this morning."

The happiness drained from his eyes and he felt as if someone had hit him hard in the stomach. "You did what?" He grabbed her by the shoulders and shook her until her hair pulled loose from its pins.

"It's all right. Stop, Eddie."

He looked down at her with an angry look, almost a threat, she thought. He knew when Emily heard this she would not bear it. Their life together would be shattered.

She saw it in his eyes, his concern for Emily and his little girls. She felt a sense of power.

She waited, savoring it, before she spoke. One day, when she was ready she would tell Emily herself, but for now, she must quiet Eddie's fears.

"Kyle is very mature. He understands everything and he knows that I am telling you. He also knows that if he tells anyone, anyone else, that I'll deny it and you will, too. Eddie, he has always admired you, really loved you. I've seen to that. All these Christmases and birthdays you've been special to him. I'll bet you didn't forget his birthday today, did you?" She looked at him, sure of his answer.

Edward's hand went to the pocket of his shirt. In the small brown box was an ivory handled pocketknife he had bought from an old man who was a sailor in his youth.

Edward looked at her for a long time, no longer angry. "Tell him to meet me at Cord's Road this afternoon around three. We'll do some hunting and we'll talk."

Before he left, he hesitated, then turned to Opal, held out his arms and laid his cheek against hers. "Thank you," he whispered into her ear. After he left she leaned against the wall crying with joy. It was the first time he had held her since the night he told her about Emily.

It was exactly three o'clock when Kyle walked directly toward him smiling. "Hello . . . Dad."

Edward's heart felt like it was swelling in his chest. When he put his arms around Kyle, he knew a different sensation; different from the feelings of protectiveness and gentleness he felt when he held Jessie or Elizabeth in his arms. He held the boy tightly a moment, then looked at his new rifle.

"Nice present from your folks," Edward said.

Kyle looked at him out of the corner of his eyes. "Having you for a father is a better present."

If only Emily could share this joy, Edward thought, but that was something she could never do.

Emily called out that dinner was ready. Jessie and Elizabeth came into the kitchen to put glasses and silverware on the table. "Where's Daddy?" Elizabeth asked.

"I saw him in the barn with Kyle," Jessie said. Emily hesitated as she ladled steaming mashed potatoes into a serving bowl. Lately she had set a place for Kyle several times a week. The boy was spending a lot of time helping Edward doing the chores he thought too difficult for the girls. "Please call them, Jessie," she asked her red-headed daughter.

Later that night she sat with Edward on the porch,

enjoying the slow movement of the swing and the smell of the honeysuckle. "Eddie, Elizabeth and Jess want to show you how they they've learned to fly Bess. Can you watch before you go back to the fields after lunch tomorrow?"

"Oh, Em, I'm sorry. I promised Kyle we'd go look at those collie puppies in Mitchell. I promised him a puppy for the work he's done for me the last couple of months.

Emily stiffened, "Weren't you going to take Elizabeth and Jessie to see them, too? " He turned away from her. "Well, Kyle asked me if we could just go alone."

"Does Gene agree about you buying Kyle the puppy?"

"What do you mean? Why wouldn't he?" She looked at him, her eyes bright with the threat of tears.

"Well, he's Kyle's father, after all, just like you're Jessie and Elizabeth's father, or have you forgotten?"

Edward stopped the swing and walked into the house. Emily sat there, knowing that he was sorry she hadn't given him a son, that Kyle filled a need in his life. She put her hands to her chest and pressed them hard against her heart. How she missed Maddy. She closed her eyes and thought of her sister.

She had visited her after Delores was born and had brought her the bracelet Aunt Alice had promised. Her own child, Jessie, would be born six weeks later. Maddy was weak but radiant. How could she have known that her golden-haired Maddy would die in six months? The tears came in a steady flow. Maddy had known. Emily got word to Edward's grandmother and Fredryk came to see his daughter. While he was there Maddy asked him to do another miniature portrait of Emily and one of herself for Delores. He made one of Maddy for himself. Maddy was wise. She told Fredryk that she had chosen a warm, loving woman to raise their daughter. She did not want her own father, David, to know about the child, not ever, so the child could therefore not be raised in Hawks Crossing. Maddy would have Judith Kelley tell her about her parents and about her grandfather and Emily when she was older and the time was right.

Maddy would have known what Emily should do to keep Edward closer to his daughters. She would have helped Emily keep from resenting Kyle and the time he took Edward's attention from her. "Maddy, help me. When we were little I was your legs. Now that you are safe with God, be my voice and ask Him to help me."

Over the fall and winter, coldness settled not only over the farm but also between Edward and Emily. Kyle had begun to take more of Edward's time and attention. Emily found him teasing Elizabeth one afternoon by tossing stones at Bess, making the hawk scream. Elizabeth was pulling at his arm to stop him. She was crying. When Emily told him to leave the shed, he laughed at her and said she wasn't his mother and not to "boss" him.

"The shed and the stupid hawk will be mine anyway. Eddie will give them to me if I ask him." Shocked by his rudeness, she mentioned it to Edward that night before they went to bed.

"He's just trying to show off." Edward said, though his eyes were sad. "He didn't hurt Bess, after all. Elizabeth has to learn to take some teasing. You know Bess is yours. It was just boy talk." She turned out the light and lay on her side, turning away from him. Tears started although she squeezed her eyes to stop them. She was feeling very much alone, even though he was so close she could feel the warmth of his body against her back.

Early that spring, on a cool, wet morning, Emily went out by herself to the wood line by the creek. She was lonely and tired—the night before she had listened to the strange two- syllable cry of the bullbats. She knew their song, these first cousins of the whippoorwill, and they always made her uneasy. Even the greenish-gold branches of the willows didn't cheer her with their promise of spring. The girls were recovering from the flu and she had nursed them alone because Eddie was busy with spring planting. She was finding it harder and harder to deal with Kyle. As she stood with her arms wrapped tightly around herself for warmth, she saw him come across the field.

"Kyle, what are you doing? It's only 5:30."

"Came to help Eddie." He knew she hated it when he used her husband's first name. "But mostly I came to talk to you. I know how you go walking every morning. I've watched you."

"Don't you think your mom and dad could use your help at home?" He looked at her with a half smile. "Gene went to the courthouse in Indianapolis yesterday and Mom doesn't want my help."

"Don't you think it's disrespectful to call your father Gene?" He looked at her for a long time.

"You don't like my coming here do you?" She looked at him in disbelief. His look and manner never seemed like those of a child. "Get used to me, Emily." She went cold at the sound of her name in his mouth. She lost her temper and slapped him across the cheek. Kyle's eyes blazed with anger. He spit the words out clearly.

"You don't get it, do you? Eddie is my father. You better never touch me again." He turned away from her and walked into the house. She knew he would wait in the kitchen until Eddie came down. He leaned out the door. "Should I tell Eddie and the girls that you're feeling poorly and went for a walk?" He slammed the door when she didn't answer. By the time she returned to the kitchen, the girls were playing and Kyle and Eddie were gone.

That evening she sat alone on the porch swing. Edward had gone to bed exhausted. The moon was bright and round as a ball, as bright as it had been on the nights when they used to dance on the porch in the moonlight. She smiled as she remembered how Elizabeth loved to watch them dance. Those days were like a dream. She walked to the shed to visit Bess, put on the fowler's glove, picked up the lure and, with the hawk on her fist, went to the south field. Pulling the hood off Bess' head, she let her fly.

For several days, Edward noticed that Emily was unusually quiet, especially when Kyle was in the house. They spent more time apart and no longer made love in the soft feather bed. When the spring rains came late one afternoon, he took the girls to visit friends so he could talk privately with Emily. He was becoming frightened by her silence and Kyle's sullen rudeness to her. And he was deeply lonely for her and for their lovemaking.

She wasn't in the house so he put on his slicker and boots and went to the shed. Bess moved on her perch nervously as she watched him. He called Emily's name a few times and then he walked back into the rain. As clearly as though someone had spoken to him, he was sure she would be at Maddy's grave. When he reached the small, unfenced cemetery he saw her sitting on the ground, her soaked dress clinging to her, her face in her hands.

"Em." He knelt down beside her and pulled her hands away from her face. "Em," he said it more softly than he had spoken to her in weeks, "What are you doing? You're soaked." She looked at him through empty, streaming eyes.

"Is it true, Eddie? Is Kyle your son?" He put his arms around her, shielding her from the rain, feeling the chill of her hands and arms.

"I love you, Em," he said and he felt her go limp in his arms. As he lifted her he stepped across the next grave, crushing some of the long green leaves of the tiger lily plants under his boots. The words Beloved Tessa, Wife of David Mc Laren, Mother of Emily and Madeleine were engraved on that tombstone. He asked once why there was no date. Em told him that her father had said that he and her mother were lovers out of time.

Doc Reuter's deeply lined face was somber when he closed the bedroom door and faced Edward in the hallway. "She's very ill, Edward. I've done what I can. She's lost a lot of weight and has been fighting bronchitis for the last month. This foolishness in the rain didn't help. We must hope that her young body is strong enough to pull her through." There was a knock at the front door. Kyle let himself in and then came up the stairs. Edward looked at him, dislike in his bloodshot eyes.

"What's the matter?" the boy asked.

"My wife is very sick, Kyle." Edward walked downstairs with the doctor and Kyle followed him. After he closed the door, Edward stared at Kyle so intensely that the boy stepped back. "You told her," Edward said without emotion. Kyle lifted his chin in a gesture like Opal's and looked directly at him.

"It was time she knew, Dad." For the first time, Edward noticed the slight, unpleasant emphasis on the last word. "You wouldn't tell her, so I did."

Edward closed his eyes, seeing the white face of his wife, remembering the nights he lay beside her with the truth about Kyle between them like a sword. Something inside him broke and he felt weak with relief. When he opened his eyes, he could not look at Kyle's face, his own face as a child. His voice was weary when he spoke. "Go away, Kyle, and don't come back to this house. Don't ever come back. You're my son, God help me, but I'll never call you that again. Just go away."

Kyle looked at him in disbelief, his chin trembling and his eyes wide with despair. Jessie and Elizabeth pushed the door open, their chattering silenced by the strange look on the faces of their father and Kyle. The boy looked at them with fury. He pushed both girls aside and slammed the door behind him. Before he left, he trampled the plants in Emily's flowerbeds under the parlor window. "It's mine. It's all mine. He'll see. They'll all see. I won't be a kid much longer. Then I'll make them see." He ran blindly to escape his pain and for the first time in his life he didn't go home that night. Instead, he stayed out in the fields and cried himself to sleep. One of the dogs found him early in the morning and still asleep, he burrowed into its thick fur. That's how Gene found him. No one ever saw Kyle cry after that night.

Rose Gold Lockets

The day they put her in the ground he freed the hawk. He looked into its wild eye as he pulled away the hood and cut the tether. The creature hesitated for only an instant, and then swept over them. It made three circles above the field near the barn. They watched it swoop over the fields, flying low then hurling itself upward. He wondered if the mirror of each fierce eye was searching for the image of a longhaired woman with her arm outstretched. Overhead the bird gave a sharp cry but no answering whistle summoned it. Bess made a final pass and was out of sight.

Elizabeth's face was upraised as she followed the bird's flight with eyes set like bits of green glass under thick lashes. Long, shining hair blew around her face and, even though its color was black instead of copper, it heightened her resemblance to her mother. At the sweet age of three, she was Emily's miniature. Her red-haired sister Jessie sobbed openly beside her, the tears streaking her face. The bird did not distract her. Three years older than her little sister, Jessie knew clearly that her mother would not return to their house that day or ever again. She believed Fr. Ryan when he said she would see her in heaven. But Jessie didn't want to wait. She needed to hear her mother's voice calling her in from play, reading stories as they cuddled in on the sofa, and laughing at the things that scared her in the dark.

She wanted to see her in the kitchen making cookies, or sitting on the swing with her father, reading or crocheting while he read the paper. Jessie wanted her mother to listen to her prayers and then to lean in close, leaving a moist kiss on Jessie's cheek and a sweet smell of lavender on her pillow every night. Mommy loved to tell her stories about when she was a girl. In her voice, so musical, so unlike other people's voices, she had told how Aunt Maddy always bought her lavender cologne and how she bought Aunt Maddy lilac dusting powder. But that soft voice was lost in the sound of coughing when Mommy got sick and the doctor couldn't make her better.

Her father reached down and picked Jessie up, holding her in his arms, trying not to frighten her by clinging to her too tightly. Yet, he wanted to hold this child with the same need a drowning man feels when he grabs at a piece of his ship broken apart in a storm. When she was born, Em had laughed with delight to see the coppery red hair and the fair translucent skin. Now, he buried his face in the springy curls and called silently to his dead wife to remember with him. With a sudden, stunning certainty, he felt her beside him.

"Mommy, Mommy," Jessie's voice startled him. She pushed away from his chest and her blue eyes were wide. "I think she's close, Daddy. I think Mommy's coming." For a wild, lost moment he believed her. She felt Em's presence as he did. A sense of absolute calm filled him, pouring into the spaces in his chest that had hurt almost beyond endurance during the interment. He had been so consumed with being Kyle's father, that he had allowed Em to think he loved her less. He thought of the nights he lay beside her wanting her and being too stubborn to tell her. He had been afraid that if he held her, she would ask him to forget Kyle. How he wished he had. Filled with shame and anguish, he had not slept since her death. Suddenly, though, he felt as though Em had touched him, returned to him, forgiven him. He smiled at his daughter.

"Of course she is, Jessie. Now you know that she will

always be near you and will look after you. You can't lose someone who loves you. Love is very strong. It stays, even after a person dies. It's a fire that goes out of them and inside you and keeps you warm." He felt a deep, warm peace.

"I feel it, Daddy, I feel Mommy's fire burning in my chest." And I feel it in mine, he thought.

Elizabeth was pulling on his coat. She had picked up Emily's fowler's glove. "Is it mine now, Daddy? Mommy said I could wear it. Is it mine?" She looked up, her eyes narrowing as she searched the skies. "When Bess comes back, I'll need it. Sometime, I'll need it." He smiled and pulled her up with his free arm. Carrying both of his daughters, he walked back to the house, and Alice, who had been waiting for them, opened the door. She was very old now, but they loved her because their mother taught them to love her. Her elegant, pencil-thin face was worried.

"Oh, you poor things. It's cold out there. Come in to the fire." As he settled the children into the cushions of the sofa, he turned to embrace her.

"Thank you, Alice," he said into her shoulder.

Her old face wrinkled as the tears slid unashamedly down her cheeks. She patted his back lightly.

"There was none like her, and I will be very much alone now that both of Tessa's girls are gone." Before he could speak, she wrapped her coat around her and moved toward the door. "There's cocoa on the stove and fried chicken and potatoes for later, when you can eat." She glanced at the girls. Jessie was quiet now, staring into the fire, and Elizabeth was running her hands over the leather glove. "They'll be all right, and one day, so will you. Believe me. I've lost everything twice in my life and still, I go on, God help me." The door closed behind her. He missed her immediately.

He brought the cocoa in Emily's favorite china cups and gave one to each girl. It smelled delicious. As they drank, he reached into his vest pocket and pulled out two small velvet pouches. "I have a gift for each of you," he said. Elizabeth's eyes brightened. "What is it, Daddy? What is it?" Jessie looked at her father without speaking. Then she asked him.

"Isn't it bad to get presents when Mommy has just gone away from us to heaven?"

"Come sit on my lap, Jessie." As she leaned against him, he reached out to pull Elizabeth up onto the arm of his chair. "In a way, this present is from Mommy, too," he said.

"From Mommy?" Elizabeth echoed. "Yes. This present is something you can keep until you are very old and go home to heaven, too."

"Mommy wasn't very old, was she, Daddy? She wasn't old like Aunt Alice." Jessie looked at him earnestly.

"You're right, Jessie. Mommy wasn't old, but I guess God wanted her to come home to heaven while she was still young and so pretty." His voice broke and he stopped to clear his throat. "But you two will live to be very old ladies, like Aunt Alice, and this present will help you remember your Mommy during all those years."

He opened one pouch and a rose gold locket on its chain twinkled in the light as it slid into his hand.

"Oh, how pretty," Jessie said. Elizabeth reached out to touch it gently, less impulsive than usual at the sight of the treasure shining in the firelight.

"What is inside is very beautiful," he told them. With his nail he opened the locket and revealed a miniature portrait of Em inside the oval. "This one was painted just after we returned from our honeymoon." Your Aunt Alice gave this locket to Mommy on the day she graduated from the eighth grade, Jessie. Edward fastened the chain around her neck.

The second pouch held another rose gold locket on a thin gold chain, which he put over Elizabeth's head, pulling her smooth hair away so that it settled around her neck. "Aunt Maddy asked someone she loved to paint another picture of Mommy for this locket. It was the last gift your Aunt Maddy sent to Mommy.

Mommy told me that Aunt Maddy's little girl has a locket like it on a bracelet. All the lockets once belonged to Aunt Alice."

Both paintings were exquisite, he thought, as well they should be. Fredryk had become a prosperous man. Collectors from as far away as Boston and New York prized his work. Edward didn't tell his daughters that Em had asked for the lockets during one of her last lucid moments. He had taken them from the small silver box that had been her mother's and opened them so she could see the miniatures that would remind her daughters of her. She had closed them, kissed each of them, and then held them closely and closed her eyes. Then, she had cried out suddenly and dropped them on the blanket. She told Edward that one of them burned in her hand. She turned away then and wept until she fell asleep. The day of her funeral, Edward felt the cold touch of fear in his stomach when Alice told him that when she bathed and dressed Em's body for the last time, she found a small burn on the inside of her right hand.

He knew that Em had a way of knowing things other people could not understand, or seeing things others could not see. She had told him once she that had seen her mother at the window of their house when she had climbed to get a bird's nest for Maddy. Another time, when the girls were sick with chicken pox, she had dreamed that her mother had placed her hands on them and the next morning the terrible itching had stopped. Even as Edward saw his daughters' pleasure at their mother's gifts, he was afraid. "I'll never take it off, Daddy, I'll keep it forever." Jessie threw her arms around his neck.

"I can look at Mommy anytime I want now." Elizabeth walked nearer the fire to see her mother's face more clearly. As she leaned closer to the flames, he shuddered. Grabbing her, he pulled her almost roughly away from the hearth. "Be careful," he said, and carried her safely back to the sofa. "Elizabeth, be careful." As he looked into her untroubled eyes, she smiled, and he knew that, like her mother, she didn't understand.

KENDRA'S STORY 1991

Kendra Caine waited for her son and Kate on the porch, her fingers tracing the carving on the arm of the rocking chair. She had prepared the fragrant chicken and rice soup that Carl favored. There was a salad of wild greens, mustard, and a few tender blackberry leaves. There was fresh bread on the table and a pot of coffee on the stove. It seemed ironic to her that she was offering solace to Emily's granddaughter.

Her anger was something she could taste. Even now with the house gone, Elizabeth, Terry, and Edward Gerard dead and Jessie in some dark world, she was not satisfied. Those things could not bring back what she had lost. Those things were gone forever. The chance to live in her grandmother's beautiful house was gone. The chance to be as loved by Sissy as Elizabeth was—that too was gone. Most of all, her beautiful Sissy was gone. The bitterness burned her throat.

She had agonized over Carl's interest in Kate ever since that first afternoon when the girl walked into their antique shop looking like her mother back from the dead. Tonight she would get her own back again. After tonight her son would belong to her again. A slight smile moved across her thin lips.

After a strained meal, during which little was said and

less was eaten, Kate and Carl sat in the small living room. Carl didn't speak, but reached for a cigar. In the quiet room Kendra's dragging footsteps made a grating, disturbing sound. Kendra stopped at the window and as she looked out she thought that they must be able to hear her angry thoughts.

"Carl," she said without turning. "I just remembered that I promised to deliver Mrs. Werner's furniture today. She'll be disappointed if the tables don't arrive. Will you do it? It will only take you half an hour and she is a good customer. Kate can visit with me and when you get back, you can take her home." Her voice held a lightness she didn't feel. Carl glanced at Kate who gave a small shrug. He kissed her on the forehead and promised to be back as soon as possible.

After Carl's truck pulled out of the driveway, Kendra sat in the chair he had vacated and leaned back. Kate looked at her with a tired smile that Kendra did not return. Instead, the older woman closed her eyes and asked her a pointed question in a tone that gave Kate an ominous feeling. "So, Kate, will you stay, now that it is over, or will you go back to Chicago?" Perhaps, Kendra thought, she might still leave and nothing else needed to be said. But she didn't believe that. "I don't know," Kate said softly. "I am still trying to take it all in."

"So you think you have learned all of it at last?" Kendra opened her eyes and gave Kate her full attention.

"What more can there be? It's over and now I must hope that Aunt Jessie will recover. Perhaps we can live together . . . I could take care of her."

Kendra took a breath, held it, and clasped her hands tightly in front of her. She stared into the air in front of her for a long time and Kate began to feel a little frightened. Kendra's voice, just above a whisper, darted into the silence like a snake's tongue. "Does Jessie still worry about that strange dream of hers about a baby that she lost?"

"How did you know about that?" Kate leaned forward in surprise. Kendra's eyes held hers in an almost hypnotic stare.

"I know because I was there." Kendra's eyes narrowed as she delivered her triumphant blow. "There was another baby."

Kate recoiled inwardly. "Why didn't you tell Aunt Jessie? She almost lost her mind thinking she had hallucinated another child. Whose child? Not Elizabeth's, because that baby died in the fire. What are you saying?"

Kendra got up slowly and began to walk back and forth. "When they called me about the fire, I locked the front door of the Pie Safe and drove to the Munro House in a state you can't even imagine. Carl was in Indianapolis at a furniture show at the fairgrounds. He wasn't coming back until the next night. I was completely alone to grapple with my fear. I knew that Sissy had agreed to baby sit with you. All I could imagine was that she had been in the house when it caught fire. My heart was pounding in my chest and tears were pouring down my face. I knew Sissy loved Elizabeth like another mother. I hated sharing all the love that should have belonged to me with Emily's child. During Elizabeth's pregnancy, Sissy often sat with you while Elizabeth saw the doctor or did the shopping. I was so afraid. If anything happened to Sissy, I thought I would go mad."

Kendra looked at Kate with misery in her eyes. "And the house. The beautiful house I had always loved and wanted—my grandmother's house—was being taken from me forever.

"When I parked the car and ran toward the house I could see the second floor had been badly damaged. Then I saw Sissy standing under the apple tree, staring at the flames. I wanted to laugh out loud for joy. Mike Collier stood beside her. He was holding you in his arms and you were struggling and crying.

"The boy turned to me with relief in his eyes. 'Mrs. Caine, I stayed with Sissy because she looks kind of funny. I'm glad you came. I'm taking Kate to our house.' He looked at the house and spoke in a whisper. 'They took Jessie and her father to the hospital. They think he had a stroke and she went with him. Sissy fainted when Ben didn't come out and they knew all of them were dead, but she seems a little better now.' My girl was standing there, white as a sheet, staring at the house."

Kendra's voice became singsong as she relived that moment.

"Mike said that they had taken Elizabeth, Terry, Ben, another person, and the body of a little baby from the house. All dead. Mike picked you up and you kept fighting him, trying to get him to let you go. I could hear you screaming and sobbing. I put my arms around Sissy and asked if she was hurt. She didn't look at me until I turned her face to mine. Her eyes were strange and staring and tears slid down her cheeks. 'Sissy,' I said. She didn't answer. She didn't seem to see me. She kept turning back to look at the house. I shook her but she didn't turn back to me. Finally I stepped in front of her and slapped her face, hard. She never flinched, even though I could see the red marks of my fingers on her cheek.

"I led her back to the car. She was like a child and did not resist. But she kept looking back, like Lot's wife. All the way home I talked to her, asked her questions, but she didn't answer. Her silence was like a river widening between us.

"Doc Reuter came to see her later that evening. After his examination he put his arm around me. I wanted to pull away because that simple act of sympathy told me that the news was bad.

'She should be all right, Kendra,' he said, not meeting my eyes. 'I think it's just shock. I gave her a strong medication to make her sleep through the night. Call me in the morning if there's no change.' I knew he hadn't spoken everything he feared.

"I debated leaving a message for Carl at the Ramada Inn where he was staying, but I knew he couldn't do anything and that Elizabeth's death would tear him apart. He was infatuated with the girl despite the fact that she was married and strange and went to the Roman Church every Sunday. I could never understand his feelings. She was nothing like us.

"I turned out the light beside Sissy's bed, kissed her forehead, and listened to her quiet breathing. When I was sure that she was resting, I made some tea. Sitting in the rocker Carl had carved for my birthday I ran my fingers over the butterflies he had carved on the armrests. I like to do that when I need to think. My boy is a genius with his hands. I like to think his love of beauty comes from me.

"Elizabeth was gone and, God forgive me, I was glad of that. Now Sissy would belong to me again. I wouldn't have to share my daughter's love. I could have all of it. The thought that Sissy loved the woman whose family had stolen the Munro House from me was unbearable. Even more unbearable was the fact that the beautiful dream of my childhood was gone and everything lovely that was in it.

"Then the idea came to me. I knew Sissy would sleep through the night because of the medication so I locked the back door and walked to the garage to get our old Ford.

"The driveway to Jessie's house was gravel and my car made enough noise to wake the dead. I told myself that if anyone was in the house, I'd say I came to make certain that the door was locked. It was unlocked and no one was inside."

"You went into Aunt Jessie's house when no one was there? Why?"

"I was sure Jessie would have some pieces from my grandmother's house in her rooms. Who would miss some little thing that would mean the world to me? They should have all been mine anyway. As I moved toward the bedroom I heard a soft mewing sound coming from a corner of the room. I stopped in mid-step and went cold. I've never been afraid to look things in the eye, so I entered the bedroom and turned on the light. I saw the source of the sound in a small bassinet in the corner. The smell of smoke met me as I bent over the baby and I understood at once. I knew the baby was Elizabeth's child even though young Mike told me that her baby had died in the fire. Someone had brought this baby to the house before the fire. But who?

Jessie? No, Jessie would have told someone about the child. If not Jessie, perhaps her father? No, he had suffered a stroke and might never recover. Then I realized it must have been Sissy. And she didn't remember because of her state of shock. Sudden warmth flooded through me and I stood looking at the baby for a long time. It opened its eyes and I felt a shock. The irises were strange, almost clear. They were the palest, most transparent gray. Tufts of pale golden hair clung to the tiny head. I felt dizzy with power. Here at hand was the chance to pay back the entire family for what they had done to me. My mind offered the alternatives. I couldn't hurt the baby, but I could take her away from them forever.

"Suddenly I knew just what I would do. I laughed and reached down to touch the little chin that was making sucking movements. For a moment I felt a deep grief and pity, even love for the hapless creature. I pulled my hand away as if I had been burned.

"I heated some milk and soaked a cotton handkerchief I found in a dresser drawer. I gave it to the baby to suck. The little thing sucked a few times, but didn't take much before falling back asleep. Using a washcloth as a diaper, I changed her and then wrapped her in a towel. The blanket and diaper went into a paper bag I discarded later. There was a tablet on the kitchen counter and pulling a pencil out of my bag I wrote a quick note. I was very calm, completely in charge of myself. Picking up the baby, I put her into a small clothesbasket I found on the screened back porch. I put the basket on the seat beside me and turned the key in the ignition. Backing out of the driveway, I headed the car toward Indianapolis."

Kate looked at Kendra with fear and confusion on her face. "What did we do to you, Mrs. Caine, to make you do such a thing? What are you saying?"

"Your grandfather stole the only inheritance I ever wanted, my grandmother's house. He bought it when her illness took all the family resources. Later I tried to buy it back from him and he refused. I had such dreams of a beautiful home and an antique shop. It wasn't much to some, I guess, but to me it was my one and only dream. He prevented it by buying the house and later giving it to Elizabeth and Terry. Now it was my turn to steal their inheritance, their child.

"There was a locket on a gold chain around the baby's neck. It was the locket my grandmother had given to Emily when she graduated from the eighth grade. She had given one just like it to Maddy for her graduation. She told me that since I never seemed to like the old jewelry she decided to give me a beautiful new silk dress and gave Emily and Madeleine the lockets." Her eyes became fixed and hard. "She gave Emily my locket, my golden locket in exchange for that worthless silk dress. Once I saw the locket around Emily's neck, I hated that dress." She stopped, her face puzzled, then went on talking to me in that flat, toneless voice. "Inside Elizabeth's locket was a picture of Emily, her mother. I took it, kept the miniature and later dropped the locket in a box of items we bought at a farm sale. It was by then, you see, just a worthless thing. I couldn't keep it in case someone remembered seeing Elizabeth wearing it."

Kendra walked to the bay window in her living room and stood there in silence, re-living that night. She remembered everything clearly but she had no intention of telling Kate what had really happened. That night she had driven to Louisville, not Indianapolis. When she found the redbrick two-story house where Sophie lived, she drove a block past it. She had bought the woman's elegant old furniture two years before. Sophie used the money to help pay for her program to help teenagers who found themselves pregnant and alone. She took care of them and helped them find good homes for their babies if they couldn't keep them themselves. Kendra could still see the note in the basket. She had written, "I am too young to care for my baby, please take care of her for me." Then, with a feeling of satisfaction, she signed the note "Elizabeth."

Kendra remembered that as she left the basket on the

porch, the child opened her eyes. In the dim light coming from a window, Kendra could see those pale eyes looking at her. For a moment, she had almost regretted what she was doing. She knew then that if she touched the child again, she would never be able to leave her. She had felt the baby was calling her. She ran to the car, drove to the nearest gas station, and found Sophie's phone number in her address book. She said, "Is this Sophie Weiss?" The answer came, "Yes, who is this?" Making her voice breathless and young, Kendra had said, "I just left a basket at your door. Take care of my baby." Then she hung up. She could still hear the click.

Suddenly Kendra felt Kate's hand on her shoulder. "What happened? Where did you take the baby?"

Kendra looked at Kate as though she had forgotten she was there. Then she closed her eyes. After a long silence, she opened her eyes and stared at Kate. "I drove her to Indianapolis and left her at St. Vincent Hospital. I told them that I found the child in the bushes outside the main entrance. While they were fussing over her, I just walked out. When it was all over, I drove home, checked on Sissy and went to bed.

"The next day the talk began. Opal's older son found a gun in the debris. The adult bodies were burned too terribly to determine if anyone had been shot to death. They identified Terry, Elizabeth, Ben and Fr. Ryan, the old priest from the Roman Church. The baby's body had been partially hidden under his. 'Everybody knew how strange Terry was,' Opal said to me. 'Elizabeth was always a foolish girl. She should have known better than to marry someone as violent as Terry. He had a temper that she thought she could help him control. She was a fool.' Everybody had an idea of what had happened. It was the common opinion that Fr. Ryan must have been visiting to arrange for the baptism when Terry lost control, shot his wife and baby, and started the fire. Terry probably killed them when he was in one of his spells. They were probably right, but I didn't care about that.

"Almost nothing was said about my Sissy. The day after I had taken the baby, I woke up hoping she would be better, but there was no change. The next night she disappeared and I found her at Jessie's house. Jessie was in the hospital for treatment but I found Sissy wandering through the house. I was afraid of what she was looking for, but when I took her hand she came home quietly. She never spoke to me again and for a long time after the fire, she was helpless. I took to feeding her and dressing her like a small child. She never spoke or wrote or read. She slept a great deal and stared into the distance. Nothing interested her. Doc Reuter said only rest and time would help her. Carl almost lost his mind because of Elizabeth's death and Sissy's peculiar behavior. He couldn't rouse Sissy from her stupor, though he hugged her and rocked her like a baby and cried and cried. Every day he left the house and went to the site of the fire. When he came back he went to the workroom behind the Pie Safe and worked on his furniture. I don't remember much of what happened then. It's as if part of my life is missing. I just remember Carl talking to me, taking care of the shop and giving me my pills, the ones to make me sleep.

"Carl said that every Sunday in St. Mary's and in the Hawks Crossing Baptist Church, prayers were said for Sissy's recovery and for mine. Sissy started in fear at any kind of fire: match, candle, or fireplace. It was clear that she'd never be able to tell whatever she knew about the fire. After a while I got better and tried to get her to go back to Sunday service with me. She ran away from me. After awhile she began to visit Elizabeth's grave and would lie beside it and sleep.

"Carl found her there from time to time and brought her home. Carl didn't understand, but he didn't scold the child. In his heart, he didn't begrudge her this little space of peace. I didn't either.

"What I have always begrudged my son was his love for your mother. Oh yes, he loved her. Like Sissy, I think he buried a piece of himself with Elizabeth. At Elizabeth's funeral we all heard her red-tailed hawk scream overhead and watched it circle several times before it flew away. Terry had given it to her as a wedding present because she never forgot the hawk her mother had flown. Elizabeth was as strange a fool as her mother had been about those birds. If I weren't a good Christian who didn't believe in such things, I'd say they were witches, the two of them. Carl looked as if he wanted to whistle the hawk back, as though she would bring Elizabeth with her. I thought it was all over. I thought over the years he had forgotten her." Kendra stopped her story and stared at me in undisguised hatred.

"Then you came into the shop. Somehow he has managed to whistle back her spirit in you. But it's too late. There's no bridge wide enough to cover the distance I've put between you. Or are you willing to forget that you will never know your sister because of me? Will you let bygones be bygones and love the son of a woman who hates you as much today as the day she stole your sister from you?" The old woman walked to the window.

"Carl's back," she said, and walking into her bedroom, she shut the door. She walked to her dresser and opened the top drawer. Under her handkerchiefs lay the oval miniature she had taken from a gold locket so many years before. She stared at the young face.

"I've done it, Emily. I've paid you back for all the things your family did to me. I've lost my house, my daughter, and all my dreams. Now you've lost a granddaughter that no one will ever know you had. I've sent the other on a wild goose chase. She'll never find her sister. We're even, Emily."

She looked at the small face in her hand in triumph. Then she put it back in the drawer. She began to feel weak, so she lay on her bed and closed her eyes. She seemed to be covered with a heavy, dark blanket that pressed on her chest. She slept.

I've put my suitcase in the trunk and I'm almost ready

to go to Indianapolis. Yesterday I drove to Bloomington to have my hair cut very short. My blonde roots are showing and I'm ready for all the dark hair to be cut away. Mike had to go to court this morning, but said as soon as he could arrange his schedule he would join me in Indianapolis. He asked me to make a reservation for him at the Westin where I will be staying. Aunt Jessie had a relapse and Doc Reuter thinks she has had a stroke. At the moment she is unresponsive but he has hopes that with time she'll improve and then he'll transfer her to a rehabilitation center for stimulation and observation. Doc blames her condition on the shock she suffered when she overheard nursing aides talking about the fire that destroyed her house. Poor Aunt Jessie. She must feel alone, the way I have for so many years. Of course, I'll look in on her from time to time. Whether I will remain in Hawks Crossing depends on my search for my sister, and perhaps later, the promptings of my heart. It will take almost a year to probate my grandfather's will, so there will be plenty of time to deal with all of that. Mike will serve as executor in lieu of his father. I know he will handle everything well.

I haven't spoken to Carl since he brought me home from his mother's house. After she went to her room that night we sat on the porch and I told him what she had said. His face remained expressionless, but as I kept talking, he stopped looking at me. His gaze remained fixed on his hands which were the only indication of his mood. They were clenched and the knuckles were white with the pressure. When I finished, the silence kept pushing the two of us farther apart. When Carl finally spoke, his voice was just audible and the words were forced.

"There are some things we can't change, some things that can't be forgotten or swept away. She's my mother and I love her, even though what she did was unthinkable." He was silent for a long time. His words cut into me like knives. "I can't walk away from her. After my father died, she lost the only complete love that she had ever known. With him gone she made Sissy and me the center of her life. She seemed to lose her balance when my grandmother died. Grandma's love was the thing that meant more to my mother than anything else. All her life she lived in the hope of sparking love for her in that cold and selfish woman. When she died, my mother knew she could never have that love. It was too late.

"The fire at the Munro House was the final blow. You don't know what my mother was like after Doc Reuter told her that nothing could help Sissy, that she might be unresponsive and distant all her life. Sissy's love and mine were the only things that kept my mother from despair. The thought that Sissy would never speak to her again made her desperate. She was ill for a very long time. Since Sissy's death, she's become morose, depressed all the time. She can't do without me now. I can't leave her. Not now. Not even for you."

The silence came again, like a hand he used to force me away from him. Just when I thought he'd forgotten I was there, he spoke again.

"I would give anything to change what happened. I would give anything to have Sissy back again, to have the chance to make you love me." He looked up at me with despair in his eyes. "I'll always love you, Kate. If you need me, I'll always be here."

He drove me back to Mike's without another word. We never touched each other or said good-bye. I just got out of the car and he drove off.

Delores called me and I told her to wait for me at the Westin in Indianapolis. She's overcome at the loss of Madeleine's journal, but I have written down all that I remember reading, and I have an excellent memory of it for I read it over and over. Of course, I'll have to tell her the whole story of my visit, but all she really wants from me is the information in the journal. For some reason I'm not angry about that. I just feel sorry for her.

I think Kendra Caine was right. In one way I am like Bess, the falcon. Someone or something has whistled me back to Hawks Crossing. The spirit of my mother, perhaps, or the call of my lost sister.

Two men say they love me. One of them loved Elizabeth, my mother, before he loved me. Perhaps it is still Elizabeth he really loves. It doesn't matter, I guess, as there is something so awful between us that to bridge it is impossible. The other man is the nephew of the man who loved Tessa, my great-grandmother. Perhaps our lives are too tangled for me to ever love either one of them. Perhaps I'm half in love with both of them. Or still in love with Drew. But that can't be. All I am certain of is that I cannot go back to my old life. What is it Aunt Jessie used to say? You can have anything in the world if you're willing to give up everything else to have it. For now, all I want is to find the small baby who has grown into a woman with translucent eyes. Everything else has to wait.

"Kate," I turned to see Mike watching me packing the last few pieces in my suitcase. His eyes were sad, almost bruised. "There's a call for you, Kate. It's from New Orleans."

"Is it Marie Celeste?" I dropped the sweater I was folding and felt a heart-pounding joy that almost left me without breath. God bless her. She always knows when I need help; she always knows when I need her. I pushed past Mike to where the phone lay on the small table near the door. Mike started to say something but turned away at the sight of my face.

"Marie, Marie, are you two back? Do you recommend honeymoons?" The voice that answered me was her mother's. I felt cold and faint, knowing from the way she said my name that something awful had happened. The air around me grew light and strange before the darkness rushed at me and swallowed me.

When I was conscious, Mike told me all of it. There had been a train derailment outside Munich. Marie Celeste and Drew had been killed instantly. Her mother called to ask me to come as soon as I could to stay with them and wait for the arrival of the bodies. She wanted to know if I would stay with them for a while after the wake and funeral since I had been the closest thing to a sister that Marie Celeste had ever had and my presence would console them.

Of course, I would go to that beautiful old house in the Garden District that I had visited so many times. Of course I would stay with the two people in the world I would have chosen for my parents. "Marie, Marie, Marie," I kept crying silently. "How could you leave me alone, where I can't find you? You were the one who kept me from surrendering to the loneliness that is always hiding near me, waiting to flow over me in a dark river and drown me." I couldn't think about Drew at all. When I did, I couldn't breathe.

Once the tears began, they wouldn't stop. Mike insisted that I go to bed. He called his doctor to get a prescription for sedatives in case I needed them. Half an hour later, exhausted by my grief, I took one of the blessed pills and slept.

New Orleans 1992

Therese opened the door to my room and put her arms around me. "Welcome, home, Katie. I only wish my Marie were running down the hall to greet you." I held her tightly against me as I felt her thin shoulders shake. She brushed her hand across her eyes and as I kissed her cheek, she smiled. My own tears slipped into the corners of my mouth and left a bitter taste. Therese went downstairs and I looked at the familiar room. The light softened as it passed through sheers billowing under blue valences. I stared at the lace coverlet on the four-poster bed that had delighted me so much when I first came to stay. On the chest beside it was a silver-framed picture of Marie Celeste and me taken before one of the many parties of Mardi Gras. The same picture was on my bureau at home. The Lilihan carpet on the floor, the embroidered, lace trimmed pillowcases—nothing had changed. Yet everything had changed.

After the funeral I stayed a month with Therese and André. Each day I visited the graves of my beloved friends and spent time talking to Marie Celeste—out loud if no one was around and in my head if someone else came to visit the graves. She seemed to be close and listening. I tried to talk to Drew, too, but it wasn't the same.

Lord knows I had always wanted to claim Marie Celeste's parents as my own, but not in this way. They wanted me to stay with them permanently and I asked her memory inside my head what she thought I should do. She had always been my guide. Of course, I didn't really expect her to answer. Not anymore. The funny thing is, she did.

On Monday morning two weeks after the funeral I woke to sunlight streaming through the glass and birds whistling in the magnolia tree outside my window. I stretched out lazily on the smooth sheets. Half an hour later I was dressed, my mint green shell tucked into cotton slacks and a pair of comfortable sandals on my feet. I walked downstairs to the breakfast room and blew a kiss to Therese who was talking on the phone. I helped myself to coffee and a croissant.

"Yes, dear, we'll pick you up at six. No problem at all. We're all eager to go with you."

She placed the phone in its brass stand and sat down next to me at the table.

"That was Ada Ranier. George, her husband, had a stroke six months ago and Ada doesn't drive, so she asked if I would take them to the healing service at the cathedral tonight. I'm more than happy to do it. It will keep me from losing myself in self-pity. I've never admired people who do that."

I patted her hand. "You're the most honest person I know."

"Why don't you come too, Katie? Healing comes in many ways. We've been through so much pain. Perhaps we can experience a little healing ourselves."

"Maybe," I said, unwilling to argue the point with her. I looked up at the television in the corner of the room. Local news was flashing across the screen. My coffee cup hung in the air when I saw his face. "Who is that?"

Therese turned up the volume and smiled. "Why that's the Irish priest who is handling the healing service. What a coincidence! We were just talking about it."

I was silent a moment, recognizing the man as the person who had sat next to me on the flight to Indianapolis.

"He's a healer?"

"No, dear. He travels with a blind healer who has quite a reputation throughout the south. One does hear extraordinary things. Apparently the healer recently prayed over a blind child who recovered her sight. If that is true, imagine what it means; giving a gift to another that you must desperately want to keep for yourself."

I nodded my head. It was unlikely, even strange that I should see the priest again. I made up my mind at once.

"Yes, Therese, I would like to go with you. Thank you for asking."

There were the usual entertainers and artists working just outside the cathedral as we followed George and Ada in their slow progress up the steps. It was 6:30 when we walked behind them toward the main altar. We sat half way up the aisle. People continued to fill the pews and I was surprised at the number of believers. An organist was playing "Come Holy Spirit," a hymn I had sung as a child. With a sudden pain in my chest I remembered learning the words from my Aunt Jessie; then there was a hum from the congregation, the assembly speaking in low but excited conversation.

Tall gold candelabra were lit just before the priest entered from the sanctuary, bowed before the altar and turned to face us. He stood beside a chair I assumed was placed there for the healer. As I looked around, I realized that there were now people standing along the wall and a few young men had lifted themselves to sit on the broad sills under the stained glass windows. Lost in my own thoughts I had not noticed that the church was full.

As he welcomed the crowd, I sat with my head directly behind the person sitting in front of me, obscuring my view. If I couldn't see him, I reasoned, he couldn't see me. He prayed out loud for what seemed a long time. Then he reminded us that God was merciful to the contrite and that we must open our hearts to healing if we asked God to send it. He spoke of the beauty of loving forgiveness as a necessary prologue to healing. Platitudes, I thought. My mind kept wandering as he spoke, riding his Irish cadences to memories of my trip to Hawks Crossing. The faces of my aunt and grandfather slipped into my mind. Sissy's haunted eyes replaced them. I didn't resist thinking about Mike, the feel of his arms around me when I left for New Orleans. The warmth washed out of me as I felt Kyle's mouth on mine. I closed my eyes, clenched my fists and willed the memory away. When I relaxed, my thoughts wandered to Carl, his face frozen into sad resignation but his eyes betraying his feelings for me. Or were they for my mother. Oh, God. Would I ever be free of that? I couldn't understand any of it. And I wasn't capable of forgiving some of it.

The people around us were rising to their feet. Putting my hand under George's elbow I helped him rise. He gave me his crooked smile and when I looked at the altar, I saw that a woman was seated in the chair. All around me the people were beginning to sing. When they had finished, we settled back into the pews. I was somewhat surprised. I had expected that the healer was a man.

The woman was young and her hair hung straight to her slender shoulders. When she raised her face I couldn't breathe. I could not make out the color of her sightless eyes but her face was unmistakable. It was a thinner version of mine. The dizziness that claimed me on the road to Hawks Crossing returned. I pressed my nails into my palms hoping the pain would keep me conscious. Pulling my eyes away from the woman, I met the priest's gaze. That's when I fainted.

When I opened my eyes, she was bending over me. Her own eyes were closed in prayer, a deep frown etching lines between her brows. We were in a small room. Judging from the vessels and vestments on shelves along the wall, I could see we were in the sacristy. The silence told me that the crowd had gone. I wondered how long I had been unconscious. She opened her eyes.

"Do you know who I am?" I looked into the beautiful, pale, sightless eyes that created a wall between us. "Yes," the response was almost inaudible. The pain in my chest was sudden and sharp. "You know about me, that I'm your sister? How?"

One slender hand reached out to me. "I know many things. Sometimes I think I know too much." Her fingers curled around mine. Our hands were much alike, even to the slight curving of the nail bed on our thumbs. "I'm sorry, Katie, that you had to pay with so much pain for my ordained work in the world."

I looked at her uncomprehendingly. "Who told you to call me that? I don't even know your name. What do you know about my pain? Oh, God, why did you have to be born to Elizabeth?"

She heard the rising hysteria in my voice, put her other hand over mine and shook her head. "My name is Sharon. I was born to our mother and blinded so that the Spirit could be released in me. That much I know. The sacrifice of my twin's life and your part in all this is not clear to me. Perhaps it was the sacrifice of our mother, our sister, our family, and you that was the price of the healing power in my hands. I can't explain it. Katie, I only know that I have brought life and the release from pain of body and spirit to so many people."

Her hands grew warm and tingly where they touched mine and I pulled away from her. "Don't try to heal me. You haven't got the power or the right. You could have contacted me. You could have made my life so different." I fought the tears that were burning my eyes. "If you know so many things, why didn't you try to find me?"

"Katie, when I was little I only knew that I was an orphan, one of many who lived in Sophie's house. Of course, I wanted my own mother and father. But Sophie told me that my own mother was unable to care for me and I doubted anyone else would want me, especially after I fell from a tree in Sophie's yard and lost my sight. I kept praying that someone would want me, of course, but no one did and I began to pray more and more often and more deeply. God was my only companion in the dark and I began to talk to Him and listen for his voice as I would have listened to the voice of my father. I became sensitive to the sound of worry or pain in the voices around me and when I touched a person's hand or face I sometimes felt a response in my own body to those feelings. At first it was just a curious experience. Then, when I was five or six years old, Jimmy, one of my foster brothers, was burned when he upset a pot of soup boiling on the stove. I heard his screams and ran toward the sound of his voice. I remember placing my hands on his face, his neck and his arm and asking the Lord whose presence was so near, to heal him. A rush of energy flowed like water through my hands. While the others watched, he stopped crying and put his arms around my neck, laughing, pain-free and with no evidence of the burn. They said the fiery red of his burns faded away as they watched me touch him. Jimmy was eight and about to be adopted by a family from Lexington. After this happened he said they had to adopt 'Sherry,' too. When they heard his extraordinary story, they decided they would take me into their family as well.

"I grew up in a wonderful family, Katie. They belonged to the local Catholic Church and I was baptized there. For the next ten years I led a happy life with Ann and Joe Reynolds and Jimmy."

"Did you ever heal anyone after Jimmy?"

"Not until Jimmy told the story to Fr. Pat Fahey. One weekend at a retreat Fr. Pat laid his hands on my head and the warmth that pulsed into them not only startled me but almost knocked him off his feet. Fr. Pat spoke with several of his priest friends and some monks from Gethsemane Monastery and they suggested that he become my spiritual director. I came to understand that my task as a healer was about to begin, that his laying on of hands was my commissioning. I've never healed anyone,

Katie, not even Jimmy. It's God who works through me. God heals.

"Fr. Fahey held a special healing service for the sick of the parish and near its conclusion, when he laid hands on those seeking relief, he asked me to do so as well. Some of those who were sick experienced healing. It wasn't long after that when he asked to be released from his parish work to become the director of a new retreat house in Louisville. My foster parents allowed me to live and work there. Two sisters of Providence were already in residence and we formed our own community. Since then I've spent my days in prayer and in the work of healing."

"That must have been nice for you. My life with Delores wasn't so nice. All I've ever wanted was to understand why they sent me away after the fire. I had the grief and you had the powers. Doesn't seem fair, does it? Why did your twin have to die? Why did you need me? Couldn't the whole thing have been worked out if you were her only child and were born blind? Why the fire? Explain all of this to me."

She stood quietly in front of me, defenseless before my anger. "Perhaps in trying to find your way back to Hawks Crossing, you found more than the answer to your childhood's questions. Haven't you found something more?"

If she's not a saint, she's a witch, I thought; then recoiled at the memory of Kendra using the word "witch" in reference to Elizabeth and my grandmother Emily. "What exactly do you think I found?" Her sightless eyes challenged mine. "Perhaps love, perhaps a way to forgive. Perhaps the truth."

"What is truth? Isn't that what Pilate said to Christ? I don't recall His answer. Do you? If you know what happened the night of the fire, let me in on it. Was our father capable of setting that fire and killing his family? Was your power purchased by being the child of a murderer? Was that the horrible memory keeping Sissy mute all these years?"

"Ah, Sissy. She paid, too, and never understood why. No,

I don't know what happened that day. Only she knew the truth and only she told it."

"But she didn't tell it. Don't you know she died without saying a word about what happened that day? She never spoke again. Her secret died with her."

She bowed her head and I saw she was crying. "Oh, Katie, of course I wanted to know what happened. I wanted desperately to understand who I was, who my mother was, and who my family was.

"But I learned that Sissy wasn't to tell me that secret. Her mother sent her with a church group to our healing service in Kentucky a few years ago. When I touched her I knew who she was. I told her that she would have the strength to write down what troubled her and that she then must put it away and trust in God to find peace."

I grabbed Sharon's shoulders, shocked momentarily by their frailty, then shook her anyway. "Sissy wrote down what she remembered? Where is it? Where is this writing?"

"I gave her a small metal box. I, I don't know if she buried . . . " She seemed suddenly very weak and reached for me as she slumped in her chair. I put my arms around her for support and felt her body slacken as she became unconscious. With panic building in me I followed the ambulance to the hospital where she was placed in a room and not allowed visitors. The old priest told me that she exhausted herself like this every few months and usually was well enough in a few days to be sent to the retreat house where she would rest and regain her vitality. I left a message with her nurse and immediately made reservations to fly back to Indiana.

Hawks Crossing
1992

I don't remember much about the drive to Paoli. My own thoughts were more real than the highway or the world around me. It was about four o'clock when I turned off the engine. I pushed open the door and walked directly to the back of the shop, to his workroom. "Carl, where are you?" He was kneeling beside a chair, his knife working the carvings on its arm. The look on his face was like having his arms around me but I went cold. "Kate." I heard hope in his voice.

"Who were you hoping it would be, my mother?" He flinched as though I had hit him across the face. He stood up slowly and faced me but made no move toward me. "That was cruel, Kate." I may have only imagined that he added, "and untrue." I turned and walked back into the shop, suddenly ashamed.

When he followed me, we faced each other like strangers. "I want to see Sissy's room, Carl. Will you let me see it?" I had the grace to drop my eyes before the look in his. "Perhaps I could come late at night when your mother is asleep so we can avoid any unpleasantness."

He didn't say anything for an uncomfortable period of

time. The words seemed wrung out of him. "Don't worry about that. She's not there. I couldn't care for her at home because she kept leaving the house and wandering. She's deeply depressed and sometimes her mind . . . " his voice broke as he struggled for control. I fought my traitorous desire to put my arms around him and let him cry. He breathed deeply and continued. "I had to put her in a special nursing home in Nashville. It's in an old farmhouse like she's used to and they're trying some drugs to help her."

I couldn't say I'm sorry, not after what his mother had done to my family. But for some reason I found myself wanting to. "So, then, can you let me see Sissy's room?"

"I'll take you. But why? Sissy's gone and what's the use of all this?"

"Can we go now, Carl? I'll tell you why on the way. Will you close the shop and take me now?"

His truck was parked in back of the shop and as he drove I told him what had happened in New Orleans. I told him about Sharon and about her meeting with Sissy and that Sissy had written an account of the fire.

"It's in a metal box, Carl, which Sharon said she meant to bury. If it's not in her room then we're too late and she buried it only God knows where."

When we reached the house I remembered the day I came for firewood and met Kyle. I could still hear his voice and see his eyes.

I hurried up the steps behind Carl. The house was cool and dark and I kept expecting Kendra to walk in and ask me what I was doing in her house. Sissy's room was on the second floor, facing the front of the house.

Carl opened the door to her bedroom, a room that extended across the entire front of the house. Its four, large windows were framed in white muslin curtains and flowered valences. A four-poster bed in one corner was built from golden oak but its beauty lay in the carvings of butterflies and flowers across the headboard. For a moment I thought with a pang about the four-poster bed in my room in New Orleans. The quilt on Sissy's bed was a bright wedding ring pattern and lace-trimmed pillows lay on top of it. I noticed that a tall armoire had served as her closet. The armoire, a chest of drawers, and a rocker were also carved in exquisite patterns. Even the desk and chair beside the bookcases hadn't escaped Carl's gifted fingers. A large, oriental rug covered part of the polished plank floors.

"Sissy must have loved this room."

"She spent so much time in it. I tried to make it pretty for her. She was so . . . " As he searched for the word, his eyes filled with tears. Again I fought my desire to put my arms around him. I reminded myself that it was my mother he loved, not me; that he couldn't separate our identities.

"Will you help me look for the box, Carl?" My voice did not betray me. He nodded and we spent a quarter of an hour gently going through Sissy's clothes and books, her bureau, the wardrobe, and her desk. We found nothing.

"Sharon said that Sissy might bury it. Did she have a favorite spot in the garden or near one of the trees?" Carl shook his head. "She liked to watch me garden but the only flowers she ever picked were lilacs because Eliz . . . because your mother liked them." At the mention of Elizabeth's name our eyes met and held. Then it occurred to us at the same time. "She spent a good deal of time at Elizabeth's grave, didn't she?" I asked. He nodded and the two of us left the room and walked in silence out of the house and to the car.

When we reached my mother's grave, I wondered why I didn't feel anything except numbness. Carl got a shovel out of his trunk and stood at the foot of the grave. "If this is too difficult, Carl . . . if you're unwilling to disturb her, let me do it." For just a moment he looked at me with a stranger's face, with an expression I couldn't read. "Kate, your mother's dead." Dead. He acknowledged that Elizabeth was dead.

Carl dug out a square at the foot of the grave and almost

immediately found the box. He held it a moment. I guess he was remembering that the last person who touched it was Sissy. Then he handed it to me and replaced the earth he had removed. There was a stone bench near the grave. We moved toward it and he sat beside me as I opened the box.

I lifted the sheets of paper filled with careful, child-like handwriting. As I read each page, I passed it to Carl.

Sissy's Story

Elizabeth lay high on her pillows, smiling at the small, red babies wrapped snugly, one on each side of her. She said she had the comfortable, tired-out feeling she remembered having after Katie's birth. Closing her eyes, she said she could hardly wait to show Katie the babies. I thought she was the luckiest woman in the world.

The only thing that would have been better, that could have made her happier, would have been to have Terry with her. He wouldn't have stayed during the birth, of course. He told her a long time ago that he could never do that. But she had longed for him to see the girls right after they were born. She said she wanted to look into his face and see the sense of wonder that was deeper than a child's, his special look of rediscovered innocence and incredulous love that sometimes took her breath. She wanted to reach out to him now, to see the surprise on his face when he saw two little babies instead of one.

Frown lines appeared between her eyes and I asked what was wrong. Terry would need to know that she was still his, she said. She had to reassure him right away that nothing between them had changed, that he could bury himself in her arms when the horrors came to him at night, that the babies were not his competition. She seemed embarrassed that she had said that out loud. I asked her what the horrors were and she just smiled.

It's nothing, he just has bad dreams sometimes, she said.

I could imagine her putting her arms around him to comfort him, but I couldn't imagine what his bad dreams might be. I asked her again.

Elizabeth said he had been struggling this last week. He tried to hide it from her but she worried about the way he sat in silence at the table while she washed the dishes after dinner. She had to speak to him several times to get his attention. He kept slipping away from her. It was a bad sign, she said. She closed her eyes and for a moment all of her happiness from the babies seemed replaced by worry lines on her forehead.

I curled into the maple rocker in a corner of the bedroom and smiled at Elizabeth, the beautiful focus of my teenage dreams whom I loved more than I loved my own mother. I thought of Katie asleep on the sofa downstairs. Little Katie had her mother's face. How wonderful that resemblance was. It made her very dear to me. Now I would have Elizabeth's two pretty baby girls to love, too.

I heard the tires of the black Ford crunching the gravel driveway. The door slammed and Terry's feet took the stairs two at a time. His voice entered the room like a sentry before his big body blocked the door. "Elizabeth." His eyes fixed on her and then became bluer as the color in his cheeks drained away. I got up and backed further into a corner, but he wasn't aware of me. He was concentrating on the two babies sharing the bed with Elizabeth.

"Surprised?" Elizabeth's delighted laugh was a bright ray of light filling the room. Looking down at her daughters, she missed his expression of disbelief and the look of fright that replaced it. He was so still that Elizabeth looked up at last. "They're just little girls. Don't look so stunned!" Her words were playful but her eyes sought his anxiously. He wouldn't look at her.

"Terry, darling, come see your girls," she said, her voice

soft, urgent. “I want to introduce them to their daddy.” I thought the room had become a panorama. I made one in school once, filling a little box with bits and pieces of paper cut to be Beth and Meg and Amy and Jo taking their breakfast to a poor family. This room was like that, a fixed scene from a book someone had written about them. Terry, so silent and unmoving, just inside the door; Elizabeth reaching out one slim hand, her lips wide in a smile, then trembling, then a pale line; my own small figure near the corner table; the sleeping babies a center of peace in the tense room.

Silence spilled from Terry in waves as his eyes moved from Elizabeth and traveled mechanically from one infant’s face to the other and finally studied the floor with peculiar intensity. Elizabeth was afraid. I’m sure of that. Both of us could feel Terry moving away from us into some strange and silent place of his own. I knew something terrible would happen if the silence continued. I moved closer to the bed, and then stopped suddenly, my skin prickly and cold. There was an awful noise in the room, worse than the silence, like the quiet, whispering sound of the wind I heard blowing one night through the leaves of the poplars that lined the entry to St. Mary’s Cemetery. I went there to prove that I wasn’t afraid and I learned what terror was. I heard Elizabeth call me. Tears slid down Elizabeth’s cheeks.

“Don’t be afraid, Sissy, it’s just Terry. He does that sometimes when he’s ill. It’s just his way of getting rid of worry. Take his hand and walk with him to the chair.” She nodded at the old wing chair beside the bed. “I can’t touch him,” I said, my own eyes filling. “He’ll hurt me, Elizabeth.”

She smiled at me. “Right now, Sissy, he doesn’t even know you are here. It’s just a way he gets now and then. It will pass. It’s something that happened to him in Vietnam. He can’t help it. Please, Sissy.” Her voice broke as she pleaded.

My love for Elizabeth was greater than my fear of Terry. He never looked at me as I walked toward him and took his hand in mine. His lips kept moving and the sound of incomprehensible words continued. I couldn't believe it when he followed me to the chair as quietly as a little child. He stood in front of it, still looking down at the floor, still muttering.

"Terry, sit down." Elizabeth's voice was loud and firm. He sat but didn't look at her or stop the sound flowing from his mouth. Moving the tiny bundle that lay between her and her husband, Elizabeth placed the baby beside her sister, then inched closer to the side of the bed. Reaching out, she took her husband's large, cold hands in hers, rubbing some warmth into his skin. "Sissy, there are some matches on top of the table by the window." She said, "Please light the small candle in front of the picture of the Blessed Mother. Sometimes, that helps him." My nose caught the sharp smell of the match striking when I lit the candle in its red glass cup. "Look, Terry, we're burning your candle in front of the Madonna. She will chase away the evil things that frighten you. She'll ask Jesus to protect you and make you safe."

"Safe?" Terry was shaking his head as if to clear it. "Yes I'll keep your baby safe." His eyes fixed on Elizabeth's face in an unknowing stare. Her streaming eyes told me she was afraid that this time it would be bad. He stood up, pushed back the chair and looked around the room, as if for the first time. The blue eyes stopped when they came to me. "Little sister, take the baby and hide in the bush. I'll come get you when they're gone. There aren't enough of us to stop them when they come tonight. They know a pregnant woman has had a baby. They know everything that happens. But they don't know there are two babies. If they did, they would . . . " Terry's voice dropped and his hands balled into fists. He closed his eyes and began to mutter profanities. He moved toward the bed quickly, reached down and picked up a baby. He put it in my arms. "Take the baby and run. Hide all night. We'll find you and stay with you until they've gone. Not too tight," he said, as he loosened my arms around the child. "Now run, you little fool, run, or it will be too late."

Elizabeth called to me softly. "Go on, Sissy. Go to Jessie and tell her to hurry and to bring Ben." Terry's eyes widened at the sound of Ben's name. "Yes, tell the sergeant to hurry. We can't wait much longer. We'll find you." I walked carefully from the room, carrying the still sleeping baby. It was like walking in a dream. As I came down the stairs, I heard a knock at the door and opened it to see Fr. Ryan's round, pink face smiling at me. The smile faded when he saw how scared I was and the tears sliding down my cheeks.

"Hurry, Fr. Ryan. Terry's sick and I'm afraid he'll hurt Elizabeth. I'm going to take this baby and get Jessie and Ben." I looked up into the wrinkled face under its white hair. "Hurry, Fr. Ryan. There's another baby upstairs. Elizabeth had twins." I ran past him onto the porch, but I couldn't leave. I crept back up the stairs after him.

The priest ran up the stairs listening to their voices. "Don't worry, little mother, I'll help you." It was Terry's voice but deep, almost whispered. "Terry, don't pick up the baby, she's sleeping." Elizabeth tried to manage a normal tone but I heard the note of rising fear that she couldn't disguise.

I could hear Terry's voice, "I'll be more careful this time, I promise. So little. You see it doesn't take much to stop the air from coming into that little nose and mouth." His voice rose. "How could it happen? I wanted to save the baby, just to save the baby. But they came early. Shhhhh. They are close. And the baby started to cry. They would have heard. I just held her a little closer to me, just a little closer, like this." "Terry," it was Elizabeth's voice, high-pitched and wild. "Terry, don't. Please, Terry." Fr. Ryan came through the door and Terry looked up at the small figure in black. He loosened his arms on the baby and pulled open the top bureau of his dresser. He fired the gun as he turned, the bullet burning the priest's shoulder and slamming into the wall. "Terry, it's Fr. Ryan," the old man said hoarsely through the pain. "Come now, give me the child and stop frightening Elizabeth."

Elizabeth screamed Terry's name, distracting him, and

the priest lunged for the gun, trying not to hurt the child between them. I ran to the doorway just as the second shot roared in the small room. At the impact of the second shot, Terry stumbled backward into his bureau, bleeding from the chest. Fr. Ryan crouched on the floor, the baby at his feet. The priest saw the uncomprehending look in Terry's eyes and raised his hand to bless the dying man before he lost consciousness himself. The vigil candle fell into the curtains where the flames caught behind the bureau out of sight of Elizabeth and Fr. Ryan. With the priest unconscious, and Terry's shirt wet with its spreading red stain, Elizabeth knew she was the only one who could save her baby. She crawled from the bed to the floor and to the baby, who was making small, mewing sounds. She picked up the baby and moved toward Terry. His eyes opened and he smiled. "Hi, little bit. Make some coffee, will you. I'm so tired I don't know if I can get up this morning. Give me five before you wake me up, huh? Love me?" She watched his eyelids close. His lips were faintly smiling. She pulled closer to him, touched his face and kissed him. His lips were warm. "Yes, I love you, Terry. Sleep now and rest." Elizabeth's voice was weak. I stood there, terrified and helpless. I think she felt the flow of blood between her legs and knew, without any sense of panic that she was dying. Still touching Terry's face, she started to pray. "Oh my God, we love thee above all things and we are heartily sorry for having offended thee. With the help of thy grace we mean to mend our lives . . . " I had heard her pray that prayer before, one Friday night when I had gone to her church with her to baby sit Kate while she went to confession. The old act of contrition faded as she lost consciousness, never knowing that the baby was already completely still. The flames, which began to fill the window, fed on the air and spread through the room covering Elizabeth, Terry, the priest, and the infant with a blanket of fire. I had watched it all, unable to move. The room was blazing and the fire moved like a scarlet and gold specter through the walls. I ran down the stairs, screaming at Katie who was asleep on the sofa. She followed me out of the house then stood in the yard looking up at the smoke pouring out of the upstairs windows. She just stood there. "Stay where you are," I shouted at her. "I'll be right back, Katie." Then I ran to Jessie's house. Jessie was asleep in a chair and it was hard to wake her up. I put the baby in the little bassinet Jessie had ready and I heard Ben's voice calling her. Jessie's father ran down the stairs when he heard the shouting. He and Jessie ran out to join Ben and together they raced toward the smoke. I ran after them.

"Hang on Terry, I'm coming, buddy," Ben shouted. Jessie, Mr. Gerard, and I were behind him, unable to keep up. I could see Katie standing where I had left her. Flames spit out of the second floor windows as we came nearer. "Oh my God, Elizabeth," Ben shouted as the image of his dark haired sister-in-law's face sprang into his mind.

I closed my eyes and prayed that I would see Terry carrying Elizabeth down the stairs. But I knew that couldn't happen. Ben was crying and I think he was afraid that Terry had hurt Elizabeth. Jessie told me that in Vietnam Ben had killed a sniper aiming at Terry outside one of the dozens of small villages they had scouted, and since then he had felt, in some deep way, responsible for him. Jessie said Ben knew Terry's weaknesses and he also knew his courage. In Vietnam he had witnessed the man's descent into the river of madness and he understood it.

When they returned home after the war, to Ben's relief, Terry had regained his self-control and his equilibrium through months of therapy. Ben had been happy to introduce the big Irishman to his steel-willed, though delicate sister-in-law. Jessie said that from the first Elizabeth had loved him, and that whatever reservations Ben had had about him seemed inconsequential in the face of her fierce attachment. Then the Vietnamese refugee family moved into Paoli and Terry reacted as though bitten by a snake. The dark moods came back and with them came the dreams and the night sweats that Elizabeth had known nothing of until then. I think Ben knew at that point that Terry had been damaged outside that little village of his nightmares and that the sight of the Vietnamese family had probed the sore. He could have hurt her. Shuddering, Ben knew Terry could have started the fire. When he was deep in his awful silence, I guess Terry was capable of anything.

Ben had pulled a blanket from Jessie's bed as he left the house and now he soaked it in Elizabeth's kitchen sink, pulled it over his head and moved through the smoke rolling down the stairway. I knew what he would see. Crawling on the floor of the bedroom, hardly able to see, he would bump into something. He would make out two figures. Terry was sprawled on the floor, and where Ben's hand touched his chest, it would become sticky and dark. Elizabeth would be lying close to Terry and next to her would be a dead baby still wrapped in a blanket.

The room was deadly with smoke and flame, and as Ben turned to crawl back to the doorway, a roof beam collapsed and struck his head.

Jessie stood by the doorway, shouting Ben's name in ever-increasing hysteria. I stood looking at the window of Elizabeth and Terry's bedroom. As the second floor roof caved in, I shuddered and my throat closed. I heard Kate's screams muffled against my legs. I knelt and held her tight, I had to remind myself to breathe, almost fainting as I watched the roof collapse. No more Elizabeth. My mind careened away from that thought and the horrible images of Elizabeth and her baby. I held Katie tighter as she tried to pull free and go to Elizabeth. Katie was all that was left of Elizabeth. How could I protect her from what had happened?

Maybe the baby I had run across the fields with would die, too. Maybe I was the reason they all died. Maybe the reason Terry got so strange and violent was because I was in their private place. If I hadn't been there, Terry and Elizabeth and Fr. Ryan wouldn't be lying on the floor all bloody and about to burn to death. My thoughts, sharp as shattered glass, hurt me and filled my head with pain. They would burn to death because of me. I had lit the candle in that room, a small red votive candle in front of the icon but I couldn't remember what I had done with the match. I couldn't remember. The cry that rose to my throat, died there. I tried to call out Elizabeth's name, then Katie's, but no sound came. My mouth was open, frozen into its round shape and my eyes were blind with tears.

"Is anyone in there?" I heard the voice like a distant echo in a cave. Twelve-year-old Mike Collier's face stared at me. I thought I heard myself screaming, but it was Katie, poor little Katie. I stooped to lift her and then pushed her into the boy's arms. I ran for the doorway of the house through a fog, my ears clogged and my head pounding. Jessie pulled me back as I tried to enter. Her face was white and mask-like with fear.

"Too late," she kept whispering into my ear as she held me and let me cry soundlessly into her shoulder. Finally the darkness I had been pushing away swallowed me. I remember slumping into Jessie's arms, sliding into a deep, empty silence.

Kate

When I finished reading, tears were sliding uncontrollably down my cheeks. Carl made no move to touch me. He was lost in his sister's pain. I stood up and, with my knees weak and shaking, I walked to my mother's grave. I felt her presence. It was the first time I had felt close to her since I was a child. I felt her great love for my father, a man so wounded he needed her as much as he needed the air he breathed. With infinite relief I knew that I was not the cause of their deaths. And I was certain that they had loved me. God bless Aunt Jessie. She had believed that I could not have started that fire. She had sent me away to protect me, to help me forget Kyle's lies. I didn't try to stop my tears. They were the tears of a frightened little girl I couldn't remember but who was buried inside of me. I cried sadly for what was lost and I cried with relief for all I had reclaimed. I was free, so free that I could even forgive and pity Delores.

I felt Carl's arm around my shoulder and turned to rest my wet face against his chest. "You don't know, Carl, you just don't know."

"Give me a chance to understand, Katie. I want to love you. Let me."

More than anything I wanted to believe that. "I'll come back to Hawks Crossing when the will is read. I want to be near Aunt Jessie and perhaps take her to live with me when that is possible. But first I need to spend some time with Sharon. Maybe I'll learn to call her Sherry. I think we both need that. But I will come back, Carl. I will come back."

As we walked back to his truck, I noticed two old graves by a low wall. Masses of tiger lilies covered one grave and spilled onto the second plot. Not far from them, under a holly overgrown to the height of a small tree, was a stone carved with images of hawks. For a moment I considered going to read the inscription but Carl's arm had tightened around me. Let the dead bury their dead. I leaned against him and we walked to the cemetery gate.

"Katie." The way he said my name made my heart beat quickly. I looked up into his eyes and saw that he was offering me something I needed. I lifted my face and his kiss was slow and exciting. It was a start.

Before I left for Chicago, I had one last thing to do. I found what I was looking for in Carl's shop and when I held it in my hands and stroked it, I knew that Sherry was right. I had found something precious in Hawks Crossing.

I drove to the cemetery and walked back to my mother's grave. I knelt there a moment, feeling the cold earth against my knees. It was very quiet. "I love you, Mom."

I placed the small brown teddy bear against the stone.

Contact Sandra Marek Behringer
or order more copies of this book at

TATE PUBLISHING, LLC

127 East Trade Center Terrace
Mustang, Oklahoma 73064

(888) 361 - 9473

Tate Publishing, LLC

www.tatepublishing.com